Nancy Drew®
in
The Moonstone Castle Mystery

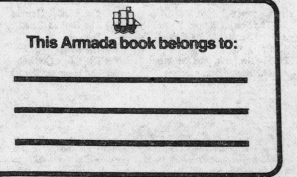

This Armada book belongs to:

Other Nancy Drew Mystery Stories ® in Armada

* *For contractural reasons, Armada has been obliged to publish from No. 51 onwards before publishing Nos. 37–50. These missing numbers will be published as soon as possible.*

The Nancy Drew Mystery Stories®

The Moonstone Castle Mystery

Carolyn Keene

Armada

First published in the U.K. in 1974 by
William Collins Sons & Co. Ltd., London and Glasgow.
First published in Armada in 1985 by
Fontana Paperbacks,
8 Grafton Street, London W1X 3LA.

Printed and bound in Great Britain by
William Collins Sons & Co. Ltd., Glasgow.

CONTENTS

Jungle Prisoners

"HURRY! Open the package, Nancy!"

Three girls stood in the hallway of Nancy Drew's home, gazing at a small paper-wrapped box, which had just arrived in the post. These was no sender's name or address on it.

"Somebody is being very mysterious," commented Bess Marvin, a pretty blonde.

"Yes," agreed attractive, titian-haired Nancy, studying the uneven way the sender had pasted on the letters and numbers of the address. "There are cut from a newspaper, and I'd guess the person was very nervous when he wrapped the package."

"Well, open it," coaxed the third girl, George Fayne, impatiently. She was a dark brunette, very slender, and tomboyish. "The sender's name is probably inside!"

Nancy, prompted by her detective instincts, was careful not to destroy the wrapping. The white carton inside was unmarked. It contained a plain jeweller's ring box. By now the girls were holding their breath in anticipation. Nancy lifted the lid.

"How gorgeous!" Bess exclaimed.

Nestled in the groove of the satin-lined case was the finest moonstone Nancy had ever seen. She stared in amazement.

"It's beautiful," said George. Then she grinned. "A mystery for you to solve. The case of the unknown admirer!"

Nancy laughed. "Anyhow, you can't tease me that it was Ned. The package was posted right here in River Heights and he's at a camp miles from here." Ned Nickerson was a college student who often dated her.

Suddenly Nancy noticed a piece of paper wedged into the bottom of the white carton. She unfolded it quickly and together the three girls read aloud the message pasted on it made from newspaper words:

THIS IS FOR GOOD LUCK FROM A WELL-WISHER. YOU WILL NEED IT WITHIN THE NEXT FEW WEEKS.

"Nancy, what are you up to?" Bess demanded. "It sounds dangerous."

"Until now, I didn't think so," Nancy answered thoughtfully. "Dad is working on a case and has asked me to help him. Girls, let's dash down to the post office and see if we can find out who sent the moonstone."

She led the way outside and hurried to the garage. Slipping into the driver's seat of her convertible, Nancy reversed the car out and the three friends headed for the post office. They had gone only a few yards when Nancy parked the convertible.

"Trouble?" George asked.

"No, but I thought it might be more sensible to go on foot. The contents of the well-wisher's note made me think somebody may be shadowing or spying on me. Why don't I go ahead and you girls follow and watch?"

"Okay," George agreed, and Bess, who was George's cousin, said, "Be careful! We'll meet you here later."

Nancy strode down the sycamore-shaded street at a fast pace. When she reached the business area, she turned into the avenue where the post office was.

Bess and George were about a hundred yards behind. Suddenly Bess grabbed her cousin's arm. "That man who just crossed the street! He's following Nancy!"

"Looks that way." George watched him intently.

The man followed Nancy into the post office. When she approached the parcel-post window, the stranger stood behind her while she spoke to the post-office clerk.

"He *is* spying," Bess declared, as she and George watched from the pavement.

The man, thin, dark, and wearing a scowling expression, turned and left the building. He went across the street and stood in the doorway of a shop.

"I think we should warn Nancy," said Bess.

George did not agree. "Why don't we follow him?" she suggested. "Then we might find out who he is and what he's up to."

"All right."

Meanwhile, Nancy had learned nothing helpful about the sender of the mysterious, uninsured package. No one in the post office recalled the person who had handed it in, or had noticed the pasted-on letters for her name and address. She refrained from mentioning the contents.

Disappointed, Nancy turned away and started for home. The strange man came from his hiding place and followed. Bess and George walked behind.

"I don't think he has noticed us," Bess remarked to

her cousin. "But what shall we do when we reach the car?"

"Let's worry about that when the time comes," George advised. "If that man was watching the house, he certainly saw us drive out with Nancy. He must have figured we went home. Let him think so."

When Nancy came to her convertible, she got in, deftly reversed into a driveway to turn round, and headed for home. The man sprinted up the street to keep her in sight. Bess and George ran, too.

As Nancy turned into the circular driveway of her home, the stranger paused. He stood very still, his head lowered, as if he were trying to decide what to do.

Bess and George had stopped also. Suddenly the man turned in their direction. He must have recognized them, because he started to run in the opposite direction.

"Come on!" George urged her cousin.

At the corner the stranger held up his right hand to stop a bus. Before the girls could reach him, he had jumped aboard and the bus was rumbling down the avenue.

"Oh, no!" cried George in disgust. "And we were so close!"

The cousins hurried back to the Drew home. When Nancy heard the story, she dashed to the telephone and called her friend Police Chief McGinnis.

"I'll tell you the whole story in a minute, but first, could you try to locate a man who is on the bus to Granby and find out who he is? He's wearing a tan and brown check suit, is thin, and scowls. He's been shadowing me."

"Yes, indeed, Nancy. Hold the line." The chief was gone nearly a minute, then came back. "Now tell me the whole story."

Nancy started with the mysterious moonstone gift and ended with the man's running away suspiciously. She could hear Chief McGinnis muttering under his breath.

Aloud he said, "I'm glad you told me, Nancy. Something's afoot, that's for sure. Watch your step. I'll call you as soon as I have some word."

As the girls sat waiting, Nancy said, "Would you like to hear about the case Dad's working on? I can tell you because it's no secret."

"But I'm sure it's a mystery," said Bess, her eyes twinkling with interest.

"Yes, and a strange one. Jungle prisoners in Africa and a baffling disappearance in the United States."

George, who was seated cross-legged on the floor of the Drews' sunny living-room, urged, "Go on!"

Nancy, her face tense, said, "Fifteen years ago a Mr and Mrs Bowen accepted a call as missionaries to a part of Africa where the tribes were restless and always at war among themselves. The Bowens had been there only three months when they were kidnapped by a hostile band and not released until recently."

"Oh, how cruel!" exclaimed Bess, who was seated beside Nancy on the sofa. "How did your father come into the picture?"

"Mr and Mrs Bowen returned to this country a few weeks ago. They went directly to the town of Deep River in Deep River Valley where they had left their two-and-a-half-year-old grandchild Joan, called Joanie, with her Grandmother Horton. The little girl's own parents had died shortly before the Bowens went to Africa."

Nancy leaned to the side and pulled open a drawer in the table by the sofa. She took out a photograph of a little girl.

"She's darling!" Bess exclaimed. "Don't tell me something happened to her!"

"I'm afraid it did," Nancy replied. "Grandmother Horton died six months after the Bowens left. There were no other relatives and the child disappeared."

"Disappeared!" George repeated incredulously.

"It's even worse than that," Nancy went on. "Nobody in Deep River ever saw or heard of the child. Her Grandmother Horton, who lived on the outskirts, never came to town after Joanie arrived—it is assumed the woman wasn't well."

"Maybe Joanie died, too," Bess suggested.

"There's no record of her death. Besides, in her will Grandmother Horton left her estate to Joanie. The estate was settled, but so far Dad hasn't found any record of a guardian or learned one thing about the child's whereabouts."

Bess gazed at Joanie's photograph. "The poor little girl! I certainly hope she's alive and the Bowens can find her."

George rocked back and forth, holding her knees. "Joanie would be seventeen or eighteen now. Pretty hard to recognize her from this picture. By the way, didn't your father talk to Grandmother Horton's lawyer?"

"Dad says he's away on an extensive trip and can't

be reached. I didn't even learn his name. Many other people who might have been helpful have either died or moved away from Deep River."

"Weren't there any servants?" George asked.

"Yes. Mrs Horton had a couple, but they disappeared at the time of her death."

"How did your dad happen to get the case?" Bess queried.

"Someone the Bowens knew suggested him. They're heartbroken over the whole thing, of course, and naturally want the mystery solved." Nancy suddenly looked out of the window. "Here comes Dad now."

The lawyer drove his car into the garage. When Nancy's tall, handsome father came into the living-room, he kissed Nancy, then said, "Hello, Bess, George. I'm glad you girls are here because I have a proposal to make."

The three friends were all attention as he continued. "Nancy, I've picked up a good clue in the Horton case from a retired luggage dealer. Some fourteen years ago a Joan Horton went from Deep River to San Francisco. I want to track her down if possible. But, in the meantime, my investigation in Deep River to clear up the business about the missing child should be continued. Would you like to make the trip—provided Bess and George can go with you?"

As Nancy's eyes sparkled in anticipation, Bess squealed, "Oh, Mr Drew! You mean it? This sounds simply marvellous!"

"And exciting," George added. "I'd love to go. May I call up Mother and Dad right now?"

"Please do. And tell them this is a business trip. All

your expenses will be paid by the Carson Drew law firm." He turned to his daughter. "Nancy, you haven't answered my question."

With a chuckle Nancy said, "Stop teasing, Dad. Have I ever turned down a case?"

George received permission to go, then Bess called her house. Mrs Marvin said her daughter might accompany Nancy, and added that if Mr Drew had not already chosen a place for them to stay, she would recommend the Long View Motel on top of the hill overlooking Deep River and the valley.

"It's delightful. Mrs Thompson who runs it is charming, and can give you girls some motherly attention if you need it."

Bess reported her mother's suggestion to the lawyer, who smiled. "It sounds like the perfect place for you girls. Could you be ready to leave tomorrow morning?"

"Yes," the trio chorused eagerly, and Bess and George hurried off to start packing.

Nancy brought the moonstone, the warning note, and the strangely addressed wrapper to her father, who studied them all carefully. "I gather these letters were cut out of a River Heights newspaper—they match the print, so there's no clue as to whether the sender is a local person or someone who came here and bought a paper."

Mr Drew was as puzzled as Nancy, and could see no connection between the moonstone and the case on which he was working.

"It's possible that some eavesdropper heard me discussing the Horton mystery the other day, and is trying to get some message across to you, Nancy," the lawyer said. "Keep alert to anything to do with moonstones."

At that moment the telephone rang. Mr Drew answered it, while Nancy waited. Presently he returned to say that Chief McGinnis had phoned. The man who had followed Nancy, then suddenly boarded a bus, had alighted before the police had a chance to intercept it.

Nancy was pensive. "I wonder if he's still in River Heights. If so, he may come here again."

"I thought of that," Mr Drew said, "so I asked the chief to send a man over to watch the house tonight."

Nancy spent most of the evening in her room packing for the trip to Deep River. She went to bed early and soon fell asleep, but around midnight was awakened by shouts of "Stop! Stop!"

The young sleuth jumped out of bed and ran to a window. Just then the sound of a gun-shot rang out through the still night.

Nancy pulled on her dressing-gown and slippers. She dashed to her father's room. To her astonishment, the door was open and he was not there!

With a quaking heart Nancy flew down the front stairs, calling, "Dad! Dad!"

There was no answer.

·2·

Mysterious Threat

As NANCY reached the bottom of the stairs, the front door burst open and her father rushed in. He went straight to the telephone in the hall and dialled a number.

Nancy stood stock-still, thankful that her father was all right, but wondering what had happened outside. In a moment he said, "Sergeant, this is Carson Drew speaking. I have a message from your man Donnelly. Donnelly has been watching our house tonight. He almost caught a prowler, and has gone after him in a car. Donnelly can't radio in because his set is out of order."

Mr Drew went on to say that the intruder had gone off in a car. "Here's his licence number." He gave it slowly so the sergeant could write it down.

When the lawyer hung up, he looked at Nancy, who still stood at the foot of the stairs. "Dad, what happened?" she asked tensely. "I heard a shot!"

Before answering, Mr Drew grinned broadly. "And you thought your old dad had met his end, eh?" he teased. "As a matter of fact, that shot had nothing to do with the prowler, Detective Donnelly, or the getaway. Somebody was having trouble with an old jalopy on the side street. It backfired just as the intruder took off and Donnelly yelled 'Stop!' "

Nancy heaved a sigh of relief. "I'm glad nobody was shot. Please tell me the rest of the story."

"Let's go into the kitchen and get something to eat," Mr Drew suggested. "That's what brought me downstairs in the first place. I wasn't sleeping, and got so hungry I came down for a midnight snack. As I reached the hall, I saw a shadowy figure sneak past the living-room window. I went to look and was just in time to see Donnelly start chasing the prowler. I caught a glimpse of the man under a street light before he jumped into a car."

"What did he look like?" Nancy asked.

Mr Drew said the stranger was thin, dark-haired, and had a scowling expression.

"Oh, he might be the same one who was following me—the one that Bess and George saw!" Nancy exclaimed.

"He probably was," the lawyer agreed. "I wonder what he was doing here."

"Perhaps trying to steal the moonstone that was sent to me," Nancy guessed.

"That might be," Mr Drew agreed. "One thing is sure—he wasn't planning to eavesdrop on us—because we were in bed."

During his conversation, Nancy quickly prepared two cups of hot cocoa. Then she brought out some delicious angel cake which their housekeeper, Hannah Gruen, had made. Father and daughter sat down to enjoy the snack and to wait for a report from police headquarters. When half an hour had gone by and no message had come, Nancy asked her father if he would mind calling the police.

"You do it," he suggested, giving a big yawn. "I admit I'd like to get some sleep. But without knowing whether or not that prowler has been captured, I doubt that I can doze off."

Nancy hurried to the phone. The report was disappointing. Detective Donnelly had reported to headquarters from a call box that the prowler had abandoned his car and fled into the woods. There was no chance of finding him in the dark.

"Donnelly is returning to your house," the sergeant went on. "It's possible that the suspect may come back. Incidentally, the car he was in was reported stolen today, so we have no clues to his identity."

Nancy relayed the message to her father and the two started upstairs.

"I suppose I should tell you a little bit more about the Horton case," the lawyer said. "Just this afternoon I received a message from a woman in Deep River whom I have been trying to contact. She was a college friend of Mrs Horton's who had been out of touch with her for ten years—in fact, until just before Mrs Horton's death. This Mrs Emory remembers she phoned the Horton house to talk to her friend about a class reunion. A man answered but did not give his name. He said that Mrs Horton was too ill to come to the phone. However, he did say he and his wife, employed there as servants, were leaving shortly for San Francisco."

"And that," said Nancy, "is where you found out that a Joan Horton went. They probably took her!"

"Right." Mr Drew went on to say that he had been

to call on the present owners of the Horton property.

"They are very nice and wanted to be helpful, but knew little about what had taken place. They had bought the property through an agent after the former occupants moved out of town. They did give me one clue, though. Soon after they had moved in, they had come upon a postcard dropped behind some old junk in the attic. It was addressed and mailed in New York eighteen years before, to Mr and Mrs Ben Oman in San Francisco. It was signed Claire."

"And you think that Oman might have been the name of Grandma Horton's servants?" Nancy asked.

"Yes, I do," her father replied. "Anyway, I think all these clues in San Francisco are worth investigating." He ushered Nancy ahead of him and began to turn out the lights.

His daughter stopped and smiled at him. "Are you sure there will be anything left for me to do in Deep River?" she teased.

"Plenty," he assured her. "And what's more, my dear, I like your fantastic intuition when you're working on a case."

The two said good night for the second time and soon were asleep. The following morning Nancy drove her father to the airport to catch an early plane to the West Coast. Upon her return, she found Bess and George at her home with their luggage.

Bess said with a broad smile which revealed her dimples, "I brought a swim suit, a tennis racket, and hiking shoes. We're going to have some fun up in Deep River Valley as well as sleuthing, aren't we?"

Hannah Gruen, the pleasant, motherly woman who

had taken care of Nancy since the death of her mother when Nancy was only three years old, thought it an excellent idea.

"If you can make people think you're there on holiday, it probably will be advisable."

Nancy was thoughtful. "I'm wondering if I should take the moonstone," she said.

At once Bess spoke up. "Please do. It's supposed to bring you good luck, and when you're solving mysteries, you can use it!"

"Luck certainly wouldn't hurt," Mrs Gruen remarked.

George was inclined to consider the whole matter superstitious. "But if you want to take the moonstone just to look at because it's beautiful, okay."

The others laughed and Nancy went to get the mysterious gift, which she put into her bag.

"Everybody ready?" she asked. "If so, let's go!"

Her own suitcases were already in the car. Those belonging to Bess and George were carried out and placed in the boot.

"Goodbye, Hannah dear," said Nancy, hugging the housekeeper. "Take care of yourself."

"The same to you, Nancy."

The three girls stepped into the car. Before Nancy could turn on the ignition, the telephone in the Drew home rang. She waited while Hannah answered it. A few moments later the housekeeper came running outside, waving her arms.

"Nancy, wait! There's a phone call for your father, but the man says he'll talk to you. It's urgent!"

Quickly Nancy jumped from the car and ran inside.

She lifted the receiver. The caller was Mr Bowen.

"Oh, Miss Drew," he said, his voice betraying nervousness, "I've just received a threatening phone call from a man. He said that if anyone dared to try solving the mystery of our grandchild, he would be walking into great danger!"

Nancy was amazed, but realized that some person or persons involved in the case must be extremely afraid of being investigated.

"Your father phoned me last night that you and some friends are going to Deep River to look for clues to the mystery," Mr Bowen went on. "After the threat I've been given, it probably would be unwise for you to go! Please, Nancy, stay at home!"

The young sleuth, by this time, had made up her mind what to do. "No, Mr Bowen," she said, "I'm not going to let anybody scare me off this case. I promise you I'll be careful, though, and not let myself be trapped."

Mr Bowen said he admired her courage, but pleaded with her to heed the mysterious warning.

"I'll keep it in mind," Nancy promised.

She returned to the car and told the others about the phone call. Before either of the girls had a chance to be influenced by Mr Bowen's advice not to make the trip, Nancy kissed Hannah again, slid behind the wheel, and waved a cheery goodbye.

Mrs Gruen stood gazing after the girls, shaking her head as if to say, "Nobody can threaten Nancy Drew and get away with it! It worries me, but I admire her courage."

Late in the afternoon the girls reached Deep River,

a small but bustling town. They easily found the winding road which led up the mountainside to the Long View Motel.

"What a gorgeous view!" Bess exclaimed when they reached the top. "You can see for miles up and down the valley."

"Yes," said Nancy, "and as soon as we unpack some of our things, I want to take a good look at it."

The travellers found the owner, Mrs Thompson, to be a delightful woman about thirty-five years old. The motel itself was charming and had a homely atmosphere. The girls were shown in to one large room with three beds in it.

"I hope you'll be comfortable," Mrs Thompson said. "If there is anything you want, just let me know." She left the room.

"All I want right now is to stretch my legs," said George, who began to do some exercising before unpacking.

In a short time the girls had hung up their dresses and put away their other clothes and toiletries in the pine dressing table. Nancy put the moonstone in its little satin-lined case in an evening bag and hid it under a couple of scarves in one drawer.

She picked up the binoculars she had brought, and asked the others if they were ready to walk round the terrace and see the view of Deep River Valley.

"Sure thing," said George.

As Nancy locked their door, Bess and George began to walk round the grounds. They were delighted to see two tennis courts and a swimming pool.

Nancy, meanwhile, walked to the edge of the terrace

from which the ground fell away sharply. She raised the binoculars to her eyes and viewed the valley and town below.

"I wonder where the Horton house is," she thought, not seeing one which fitted the description her father had given.

Suddenly Nancy noticed that a thunderstorm was brewing. For a few moments she watched the scudding black clouds. Then, as she swept the binoculars downwards towards the river, she focused directly on an unusual sight.

"A castle!" Nancy murmured to herself.

The building stood on an island. It was two storeys high and had a turret at one end. Round three sides was a dry moat with a drawbridge, which was up, and formed part of the castle wall. When Bess and George joined her, they took turns using the binoculars, so that they too might view the castle.

"How absolutely fascinating!" Bess exclaimed. "To think of a real castle way out here!"

"I suppose the moat was once filled with water that came from the river," George commented. "While we're here, let's go down and see it at close range."

Nancy nodded agreement. Taking the glasses again, she studied the building and grounds, then said, "The surroundings look pretty wild. I wonder if anyone lives there."

The three girls were so intent on the view that they had not noticed that the storm clouds were coming closer. A strong gust of wind suddenly blew their skirts.

"It's going to rain!" said Bess. "We'd better go inside."

As they started back, the girls passed a huge oak tree. At that instant a bolt of lightning ran down one side of the trunk. A terrific cracking noise followed. The ground vibrated, giving Nancy and her friends a tingling sensation.

"The tree's going to fall!" Bess screamed.

· 3 ·

A Strange Inquiry

THERE was a tremendous crash behind the girls. The great oak had split in two, the outermost branches of the falling section barely missing Nancy and her friends.

"Goodness! That was a narrow escape!" said George, catching her breath. "I feel numb."

"So do I," said Nancy. "It's a good thing we weren't any closer to that bolt! We might have been struck!"

"I'm a wreck," Bess declared. She kept on going, however, towards the motel.

As the three girls rushed inside, there was a bright flash of lightning. It was followed by a deafening roar of thunder.

"There's no rain!" said Bess, quavering. "What's the matter?"

Nancy answered her, "I guess this is what's known as a dry storm. They're the worst kind."

In a few moments, however, it began to rain. The curtain of water was so thick that one could not see more than ten feet ahead through the windows. As they watched the storm, Mrs Thompson came to the girls' room to inquire if they were all right.

Nancy assured her that they were, but confessed that the bolt of lightning and the crashing tree had given them a scare. "I'm terribly sorry your lovely oak is ruined," she said sympathetically.

"I'm sorry too," the motel owner replied, "but the ruined side is away from the motel. Perhaps it can be fixed so that it won't be too noticeable."

"Do you often have storms like this?" Bess asked.

Mrs Thompson said it was the first one since she had taken over the management of the motel. "But then I'm new to the community. I've been here less than a year."

"Then perhaps you don't know much about the castle I saw down in the valley," Nancy remarked. "It looks like an intriguing place."

Mrs Thompson smiled. "I have no doubt it is. Since I came here I've been so busy that I haven't had time to learn much of the local history. But"—she paused for a moment, her eyes twinkling—"I suggest that if you want to learn anything about Deep River or Deep River Valley, you talk to Mrs Hemstead. She's the mother of the owner of the tearoom in town called the Brass Kettle."

The three girls laughed and George remarked, "You mean she's the town busybody?"

"I guess that's a good name for her," Mrs Thompson answered. "She prides herself on not missing a thing that's going on."

Nancy was listening intently. Here was somebody who might know something about Mrs Horton's grandchild!

"Let's have supper at the Brass Kettle," she said to

the girls, who realized the significance of her suggestion.

They waited until the rain had stopped, then left for the quaint village. Nancy drove the full length of Main Street, looking left and right for the Brass Kettle. Not seeing it, she turned back, remarking, "The tearoom must be on a side street."

As they drove along, pausing at each junction, Nancy noted the lettering on two different office windows. Both offices were occupied by solicitors. "I wonder if one of them was the lawyer who settled the Horton estate, and if so, whether he has returned from his trip," Nancy mused.

She also noted that there were two banks, and made up her mind to visit all four places the next day, and find out what she could.

Suddenly George called out, "I see the tearoom. Stop! Turn to the right!"

Nancy reversed, then drove down the side street. The Brass Kettle was two doors from the corner.

The place was attractive. In front of the old-fashioned white house with a centre entrance was a lovely garden of flowers, enclosed by a white picket fence.

The girls entered the restaurant. The interior was just as quaint and attractive as the exterior. On the left of the centre hall was a waiting room with a high-backed sofa and straight chairs. Several hanging shelves with knick-knacks decorated the walls. Over the fireplace, in an elegant gilt frame, was the portrait of a distinguished-looking elderly man with white hair and a long beard. Thick carpeting, with a large flower design, blended perfectly with the other furnishings.

Nancy and her friends noted all this in a quick glance. Their attention focused on an old lady seated in an antique rocking chair. Her black silk dress was severe and the neckline edged in ruching. Talking to her was a short, stout man, his back to the girls.

As the girls paused, they heard the old lady say to him in a high-pitched voice, "The name's Drew, you say? I'll let you know."

Bess and George each grabbed one of Nancy's arms. Did the stranger perhaps mean Nancy or her father?

Instantly Nancy decided it might be wise to stay out of sight. Pulling the girls to one side, she whispered, "I'll go into a back corner of the tearoom. Find out what you can, and if you have to give names, just use your own. Don't mention mine or let on I'm here."

Nancy hurried from the doorway and found a table well hidden from the waiting room. Meanwhile, Bess and George dawdled in the hall, hoping to hear more and to get a good look at the man. Eventually he moved into view.

Bess rearranged her hair several times, then took out a mirror and spent a few moments freshening her make-up. George, whose hair was short and close cut, found it difficult to change her hair style, so she, too, freshened up. Then she pretended to be having difficulty brushing some imaginary dirt off her blouse.

Suddenly the man said to the elderly woman, "I must meet Miss Drew. I have something very valuable to give her."

Bess jumped. It might be a gift for Nancy!

"Very good, Mr Seaman," the woman replied.

Bess whispered to George, "We ought to call Nancy and let him give her this valuable thing if she's the right Drew."

"No!" George said in a low but firm voice. "If he means Nancy, I don't believe there's any gift. Bess, you go in with Nancy and tell her what happened. I'm going to follow that man and see what I can find out."

Her cousin demurred for a moment, but George was insistent. "Don't worry. I'll be careful," she promised. "I'll just see where he goes."

Satisfied, Bess turned into the tearoom and walked to the table where Nancy was seated.

As Mr Seaman said, "Goodbye Mrs Hemstead . . . I'll be seeing you," George turned her back to the waiting room and put her head down as if searching for something in her purse. The man came out and immediately left the restaurant. George followed.

The stranger walked quite a distance up Main Street. His pace quickened. So did George's.

"Where in the world is he going?" she asked herself. "I wonder if he knows I'm following him and is trying to throw me off the track."

Nevertheless, she strode on determinedly. Finally, at the very edge of town, she noticed a parked car. As the man approached it, the door swung open and he jumped inside. Instantly the car drove off.

George was not close enough to do any more than get the licence number of the dark car and note that the driver was a woman. It was too dark to distinguish anything about her. The young sleuth turned back.

At the tearoom Nancy and Bess ordered their meal.

They ate slowly, thinking George would return at any moment. They finished eating and still George had not returned. Both girls became alarmed. What could have happened to George?

"I never should have let her go alone," Bess chided herself. "George takes such wild chances. Goodness only knows what she may have gotten into."

Nancy was afraid that Mr Seaman, thinking George was following him and not wishing to be found out, might have harmed her.

"George may be a prisoner this very minute!" Bess said fearfully.

Though Nancy agreed, she remarked, "George knows how to take care of herself. Just the same, I think we should look for her."

The girls quickly paid their bill and left the tea-room. They looked up and down the side street, then walked to Main Street. George was not in sight.

"That Mr Seaman may have been the man who phoned the Bowens," Bess said. She was almost in tears. "M-maybe that threatened danger is already in progress!"

As the girls wandered aimlessly along the street, a little boy, who had been playing on the pavement, smiled at them.

Nancy returned his smile and said, "We're looking for a friend of ours," she explained, then described George. "Did you see a girl like that anywhere?"

"Oh, yes," the little boy answered. He pointed. "She went that way."

With this slim clue, Nancy and Bess hurried in the direction the little boy had indicated. They came to the end of town, but their search had yielded nothing. Discouraged, they turned back.

"Oh, I just *know* George has been kidnapped!" Bess moaned in panic.

·4·

Nancy's Impersonation

"I NEVER should have given you girls that assignment," Nancy said. "If something has happened to George, I can't forgive myself."

Bess was in tears. She and George had many little misunderstandings and sometimes found fault with each other, but the two girls were very close. The thought that George might be a prisoner was almost too much for Bess.

"We must find her!" she said, a catch in her voice.

"If we don't get a lead on George in a few minutes, we'll tell the police," Nancy agreed. "Let's go back to the tearoom and find out from Mrs Hemstead where Mr Seaman lives. Then we'll go right to his house."

As the girls hurried along, Nancy added, "Bess, I'd still like to keep my identity here a secret. Do you remember the play I was in where I took the part of the shy girl—with the high-pitched voice—named Irene Insbruck?"

"I'll never forget it," said Bess.

"Well, I'm going to become Irene while I'm doing my sleuthing here," Nancy announced.

When the girls reached the tearoom, it was about to close. Mrs Hemstead still sat in her rocking chair, swaying gently back and forth and humming a hymn.

Despite the gravity of the situation, Bess could hardly keep her face straight as Nancy introduced herself in a voice pitched almost an octave higher than her normal one. Then she asked, "I understand you know almost everyone in town. Could you tell me where Mr Seaman lives?"

Mrs Hemstead leaned forward and gave a little chuckle. "Are you his girl friend?" she asked, as if she were latching on to a possible bit of gossip.

Nancy did not have a chance to answer. Mrs Hemstead, presuming this was the case, prattled on. "Nice man, Mr Seaman. Reliable-like." She winked. "That's the kind of man a girl ought to have for a husband."

In the pause that followed, Bess felt she should say something to carry on the pretence, so she remarked, "Mr Seaman really ought to diet, though. Irene prefers thin men."

Mrs Hemstead laughed aloud and turned to Nancy. "After you're married to him, you can put him on a diet," she said, giving Nancy another wink.

Nancy, playing the game, laughed too. "Right now I'm only interested in learning where his house is. He never said."

"Well, now, I can't tell you that," the old lady said. "It's somewhere out of town, but he never told me where it is."

Nancy showed her disappointment. She changed the subject abruptly. "Mrs Hemstead, do you think I would like it here in Deep River?"

"I don't see why not. I've lived here all my life and look at me—hale and hearty yet!"

The impersonator acted unconvinced. "I've heard some strange things have happened in this town," she said.

"Oh, it's not bad." Mrs Hemstead shrugged. "Of course—" There were a few moments of silence, then the old woman brightened, sat up straight, and rocked back and forth furiously. "Of course, there's the castle. Too bad it was abandoned. It was once a beautiful place—the show place of Deep River fifty years ago."

"Who owned it?" Nancy queried in her "Irene" high-pitched voice, which almost matched the tone of Mrs Hemstead.

"Some foreigners built it and lived there until it became haunted," Mrs Hemstead answered.

"Haunted?" Bess repeated.

"I'll say it was," Mrs Hemstead replied. "The folks never finished building the castle—it was to have another turret—and finally abandoned it. There was one tragedy after another—a child drowned in the moat, a man got hoisted on the drawbridge and was crushed—"

"Oh, please," said Bess, "don't tell us any more."

Mrs Hemstead was not to be stopped. She said that no one had lived in the castle for many years, but the taxes on it were paid by someone living in Europe. "So the town can't do anything with the place. The county can't do anything with it, either. The State Police look it over once in a while to see that everything is in order out there."

Mrs Hemstead suddenly pointed to an ancient framed map hanging on the wall. "Look at that," she directed. "If you look closely, you'll see that Deep

River Valley was originally ca''   ..oon   . Valley. Nobody seems to know why the name was changed. I guess the people who lived in the castle knew this and liked the name, because the' .lled their place Moonstone Castle."

At this bit of information Nancy and Bess looked at each other. This was the second time in two days that "moonstones" had come to their attention. Was there any connection between Moonstone Castle and the gem which had been sent so mysteriously to Nancy?

"Speaking of strange things," Mrs Hemstead said reminiscently, "there's the case of Mrs Horton."

Nancy and Bess could hardly conceal their excitement.

"Horton?" Nancy repeated.

"Yes," said Mrs Hemstead. "Her place was quite far out of town. She never was sociable, so folks around here didn't know her very well. She never mingled much, and after her son and daughter-in-law died, nobody ever saw or heard from her again until just before her death."

"What happened to her?" asked Nancy.

"Well, it was like this," Mrs Hemstead related. "Just at the time her son died, a couple of servants she had went off suddenly, and a new couple came there. After that, food was always delivered to the house, but the money for it was left outside. The delivery men who went out there never saw anybody.

"Talk got around that Mrs Horton had become eccentric. Personally, I don't know who was the queerest—Mrs Horton or those servants she had. Why, do you know at the time of her last illness, they actually called in an out-of-town doctor, and when she died, the servants sent for an out-of-town undertaker? And what was even worse, the funeral was private. Not a soul in this town knew about it until it was over."

Nancy and Bess did not comment. Numerous questions raced through their minds. Bess, impulsively, suddenly blurted out, "What happened to the little grandchild who was staying with Mrs Horton?"

The instant she had asked the question, Bess was sorry. To her and Nancy's relief, however, the old lady did not seem to think the question out of order.

"*Little grandchild?*" she remarked. "If Mrs Horton's son had a little child, nobody around here knew it." The woman chuckled. "You can bet your life, if any child *was* out there, I would have heard about it!"

The two girls made no comment, for, at that moment, Mrs Hemstead's daughter came into the room. "Mother," she said, "it's time for bed. You've had quite a day."

Nancy and Bess left at once. They realized they should continue their search for George. When they reached the street, they turned in the direction where they had seen police headquarters.

Their hearts and minds full of worry, the two girls hurried along in silence. As they passed a well-lit café, crowded with young people, they suddenly heard a familiar whistle.

George was signalling to them from inside the shop!

"Oh, thank goodness!" said Bess in relief.

Nancy felt that a great weight had been lifted from her as she and Bess hurried inside.

"You've given us the worst scare of our lives! What—" Bess started to scold her cousin.

"I was just going to phone the tearoom to tell you where I was when I saw you coming," George told the girls. "Come and sit down with me while I finish eating and I'll tell you everything that happened." They listened attentively to her account of following Mr Seaman and his going off in a car driven by a woman.

"I started back to town. Halfway here, I was sure a man was trailing me. By this time, it was too dark to see him very well, but he *wasn't* the man I followed from the Brass Kettle."

"What did he look like?" Bess asked.

"He was very thin. In fact, I think he was the same man who was following you in River Heights, Nancy," said George. Suddenly she looked out of the window and cried, "There he goes now! Look!"

Nancy and Bess dashed to the window as the man hurried up the street.

"That man looks familiar to me!" Nancy said excitedly.

· 5 ·

The Spooky Drawbridge

"Do you know that man?" George queried.

Nancy thought hard but could not remember who he was. "His face certainly does look familiar. Maybe it will come to me later. Let's follow him and see if we can find out who he is."

George's meal was quickly paid for, and the girls hurried to the street. The stranger for whom they were searching was nowhere in sight. The young sleuths peered into various shops that were still open, and looked up and down side roads. The man had vanished.

"Well, we may as well go home," said Nancy. "I confess I'm ready for bed."

"Me, too," said Bess, yawning.

On the way back to the motel, Nancy said she would like to visit the castle early the next morning. "That place intrigues me. It probably holds a mystery."

"I thought we were trying to find Joanie Horton," Bess spoke up. "Don't tell me you think she's being hidden in the castle!"

Nancy laughed. "No, not after all these years. I suggest we go to the castle before breakfast. Then we can start our sleuthing at the banks and those lawyers' offices."

The three friends were up early. On the way to the parking area they stopped to gaze at the view of the valley. The sun was not very high yet and sections beneath the hills were in deep shadow. The castle, however, stood out clearly.

Suddenly Nancy called out excitedly, "Girls, the drawbridge is down now!"

"But the place is supposed to be empty!" Bess said. "It's positively spooky!"

The others agreed and stared at the spot, puzzled. Why was the bridge in this position? Who had lowered it?

"Maybe it just fell," Nancy suggested.

"Could be," George said. "Or maybe some sightseers were there, walked over the dry moat, and then let the drawbridge down so that they could go back across it."

"It's a logical explanation," Nancy agreed. "Well, shall we go?"

The girls climbed into Nancy's convertible and she wound down the hillside to the town. Not many people were in evidence in Deep River and the visitors knew the restaurants would not be open yet.

"I know I'm going to be famished before we get back," Bess declared.

"It won't hurt you," said George, surveying Bess's plump figure.

Bess made a face but did not retort. She sat in silence as Nancy covered mile after mile. "I had no idea the castle was so far from the business district," she remarked.

Finally they reached the grass-overgrown lane which led into the property.

"Tyre tracks!" George pointed out. "Somebody has been here recently."

Nancy parked at the side of the lane some distance from the moat. The tracks of the other car went on to the drawbridge. "I think we'd better proceed on foot," she said. The girls got out and walked forward.

"I'm glad the bridge is down," said Bess. "I'd hate to plod deep into that moat and up again on the other side."

Suddenly Nancy, who was in the lead, cried out, "There's water in the moat! A lot of it!"

The cousins hurried forward to look over the edge with Nancy.

"It looks deep, too," she added. "It's not just rain water."

Bess was fearful. "Who put it in if nobody's living here?"

Nancy admitted that she was puzzled but was eager to continue the trek over to the castle itself. Before the girls could start, the bridge began to rise!

"Oh!" Bess screamed. "The castle *is* haunted! A ghost must be raising the drawbridge!"

"Don't be silly!" George scolded her. "The townspeople and the police may think this place is unoccupied, but it's my guess somebody is hiding here."

Nancy, who long ago had made it a rule never to side with either of the cousins when they were disagreeing, said, "One thing is sure. If we expect to get across now, we'll have to swim. Let's go back to town, have breakfast, do our calling at the banks and lawyers, then come back here wearing our bathing suits."

Bess did not comment on the suggestion, but it was

evident from the expression on her face that she did not relish the adventure. As they walked to the car, the three friends kept turning around to see if they could catch a glimpse of anyone on the castle grounds. Nobody appeared. The place seemed to be deserted.

"I wonder if more than one person is hiding in the castle," said Nancy.

George remarked that there must be more than one person. The bridge had been let down for a car to go over. And someone inside the castle walls apparently had pulled up the drawbridge.

"Oh, dear!" said Bess. "This is getting terribly complicated. Why don't we leave the castle out of our sleuthing?"

The other girls did not answer her. Both Nancy and George were curious to see what was going on in the abandoned spot. Why had water been put into the moat and by whom? Had it been done to keep people out of the castle?

As soon as the girls reached Deep River, they went to the Brass Kettle, but it was not open. They turned and walked back to the main street and went into a restaurant. Their breakfast proved to be delicious and Bess's good humour returned.

By the time the girls had finished eating, the shops and offices were open. Nancy headed for the Deep River National Bank.

Bess and George were always interested in observing Nancy's sleuthing procedures. They often wondered whether it was her charm, her straight-forward manner, or her businesslike approach that unfailingly gained her entrance to offices of officials. Now, with little explanation on her part, the girls were ushered into the manager's office.

Mr Kleat was a pleasant man, but one who repeatedly was interrupted by telephone calls and messengers. He listened attentively, however, to Nancy's request for information about the deceased Mrs Adelaide Horton.

"I'm afraid there is little I can tell you," the man replied. "I knew Mrs Horton only slightly. One day she came in and closed both her current and her savings accounts. Then she went to her safe-deposit box and removed the contents—apparently securities."

"She gave no explanation?" Nancy asked.

"None whatever. She was not a talkative person. Furthermore, we never question what our clients do. Of course we were sorry to lose her accounts."

"How long ago was it?" Nancy queried.

Mr Kleat thought for a few moments, then said, "I can't remember exactly how many years ago, but it was a few months before her death."

At that moment Mr Kleat's buzzer sounded. He answered and said, "All right. Put him on." The manager turned to the girls. "I'm sorry, but you'll have to excuse me now. I have an important long-distance call."

Nancy stood up hastily and thanked him. She hurried from the room, followed by Bess and George.

When they reached the pavement, George asked, "Nancy, do you think that you learned anything important?"

"Indeed I do. I've had a feeling all along that something strange was happening between Mrs Horton and the couple who worked for her. I'm beginning to think that maybe the servants were using some hypnotic influence over Mrs Horton to get her money and securities away from her."

"How perfectly dreadful!" Bess commented.

Nancy walked up the street, telling the girls she was going to visit the other bank in town. At this institution the girl detective was told a similar story to the one she had just heard, but the information came from the head cashier. He was the only person who had been working at the bank fifteen years before.

This man was a little more talkative and revealed the fact that Mrs Horton was considered to be wealthy. "I believe she left everything to a granddaughter," he said, "but the details have slipped my memory."

Nancy was sorry to hear this, because for a moment she had hoped that the man would supply a helpful clue. He smiled. "Mrs Horton never talked about her personal affairs to anyone—she didn't seem to want a soul to know her business."

Nancy, realizing that the cashier could throw no further light on the mystery, thanked him and the girls left the bank. Their next stop was at one of the law offices. Here the young sleuths learned nothing—the two lawyers who shared the office had been in town less than five years and had never heard of Mrs Horton.

At the next lawyer's Nancy had a little better luck. The man had heard of Mrs Horton, and although he knew nothing about her personally, he said, "I believe a Mr John Wheeler, who is now retired, took care of her estate."

"Does he live in town?" Nancy asked eagerly.

"Yes. On Victoria Street. I don't know the number of the house, but you can't miss it. On the front lawn there's a huge statue of a dog."

As the girls hurried towards Mr Wheeler's home, Nancy wondered if this was the man to whom her father had referred and who was reported to be out of town. She fervently hoped he was back!

To her delight, Mr Wheeler had returned and he welcomed the girls cordially. He was about seventy years old, but very spry looking.

"It's rare that even one young lady comes to call on me," he said with a lilt in his voice. "To have three all at once—and such attractive ones—is a great pleasure indeed. Do come in and sit down."

The girls seated themselves in the spacious, beautifully furnished living room. Nancy apologized for the intrusion, then introduced herself as the daughter of Carson Drew, the lawyer.

"I believe you settled the estate of Mrs Adelaide Horton?" Nancy said questioningly.

"Yes, I did."

Nancy said that her father had come to Deep River looking for Mr Wheeler, but had learned he was out of town.

"My father had to make a business trip, so he asked me to come up here and make some inquiries."

"And what is it you want to know?" Mr Wheeler asked, his voice now showing a note of suspicion.

"It's about Mrs Horton's granddaughter to whom she left her money."

"Well?" Mr Wheeler lifted his eyebrows. "Everything was in order. Just before Mrs Horton's death she

eft a note giving the address of her granddaughter. The
girl was notified and came here from New York City.
Her lawyer accompanied her. She had full credentials
o prove who she was." After a pause Mr Wheeler
added, "So she inherited Mrs Horton's estate. That's all
here is to the story."

"But she couldn't have!" Bess blurted. "She was
only three years old!"

Mr Wheeler smiled affably. "Oh, no," he said. "She
was twenty-one."

Nancy, Bess, and George were stunned. "Where is
Joanie Horton now?" Nancy asked.

"I have no idea," the retired lawyer answered.

Nancy's mind was in a whirl. If Mr Wheeler's story
were true, who were the Mr and Mrs Bowen that had
come to Mr Drew? Were they impostors? If so, what
was their scheme? On the other hand, Nancy reflected,
maybe a great hoax had been perpetrated and an
impostor had received the estate.

A similar thought went through George's mind. She
asked abruptly, "Mr Wheeler, weren't you suspicious
about that girl who claimed to be Joanie Horton?"

The former lawyer's face instantly turned red, then
almost purple. He jumped from his chair and in anger
shouted, "How dare you, young lady! The idea of
questioning my integrity! I suggest that you and your
friends leave at once!"

· 6 ·

A Legal Tangle

"WHY, Mr Wheeler, I didn't mean—" George broke in. "Please forgive me."

The retired lawyer, mollified by George's apology took a deep breath.

"Perhaps I should explain," Nancy said. "We heard that Mrs·Horton had a little grandchild staying with her. But no one in Deep River seems to know anything about her. Your story startled us."

Mr Wheeler finally calmed down. "I will outline the circumstances," he said, seating himself again. "When I was called in, Mrs Horton was already dead. Only the doctor and the undertaker were there, but they showed me several notes left by her on a bedside table, along with a couple of signed cheques. All were in the old woman's handwriting. One said the granddaughter mentioned in her will lived at a certain address in New York City. Another note said she desired a private funeral. A third requested that since Joan's parents were not living, I was to take charge of everything.

"Accordingly, I notified the granddaughter who came here with a lawyer and a couple. They were friends. Joan had with her a birth certificate, a copy of the marriage licence of her parents, and letters from her

48

grandmother. The identification seemed bona fide."

Bess inquired, "The age of the grandchild and a guardian were not mentioned in the will?"

"No," Mr Wheeler answered. "By the way, I did not draw the will. The lawyer who had and the witnesses who had signed it were not living."

"Was there a large estate?" Nancy queried.

The retired lawyer said there had been very little cash in Mrs Horton's home safe, but he had found many securities there. "All of them were transferred to Joan," he explained. "After she left the Horton house, I never heard from her again."

"Did she sell the property?" George spoke up.

"Yes. It was purchased by neighbours, but it has since been sold to other people."

"What was the name of the couple who worked for Mrs Horton just before her death?" Nancy asked. Mr Wheeler said he did not know.

All this time Nancy had been studying the elderly man's face. It was an enigma to her. Was he completely honest or was he involved in a crooked deal regarding the will?

George asked, "Those notes you were given—could they possibly have been forgeries?"

The retired lawyer, instead of becoming angry over the question, looked troubled. "I most certainly hope not," he said.

"Did you keep the notes?" Nancy asked.

"No, I didn't. As a matter of fact, I laid them down at the Horton house and they disappeared. I assumed someone had thrown them away, thinking they were no longer of any use."

Nancy stood up. She felt that the girls had gleaned all the information possible from Mr Wheeler, who appeared genuinely upset.

"I'm sorry we disturbed you," said Nancy. "Thank you very much for this information. I'll pass it along to my dad. Probably he will be in touch with you when he returns home."

Bess and George said goodbye, but Mr Wheeler did not rise. He seemed stunned and his thoughts far away. Nancy wished she were a mind reader! Had Mr Wheeler told all the facts?

The girls let themselves out by the front door and started for the car. "That was really something, wasn't it?" Bess remarked.

"I don't know who was more stunned—Mr Wheeler or me," said Nancy. "Do you realize what this means, girls? If this whole thing was a grand hoax, and someone got away with Mrs Horton's estate, there's no chance of the real Joanie Horton's getting it, or even of being found."

"And don't forget," Bess added, "that we haven't learned one single thing about the three-year-old child named Joanie Horton. It looks as if she never existed!"

"It sure is a mystery," said George, as the girls climbed into the car.

After lunch they returned to the motel. Nancy went at once to telephone her father. She learned, however, that he had left the San Francisco hotel, but was expected back in a few days.

Nancy next phoned Hannah Gruen. When the housekeeper heard the latest developments in the case, she was alarmed by the news.

"There may be more danger in this mystery than you bargained for, Nancy," she said. "If your father should phone, I'll give him your message and I'm sure he'll get in touch with you." The kindly woman begged Nancy to use extreme caution as she proceeded in her sleuthing.

"Don't forget," Nancy reminded her with a chuckle, "that the moonstone I brought is supposed to bring me good luck!"

"Moonstone, bah!" Mrs Gruen said. "Use your good common sense and you'll be better off!"

As Nancy said goodbye, Bess came up to her and announced she would like to offer a suggestion. "Don't you think you ought to get in touch with the Bowens and tell them the whole story?"

Nancy shook her head. "I'll call them, but I won't tell them what we've learned. It's possible that *they* may be the phonies. I'm sure I can't imagine what their game would be after all these years, but Dad says never take anything for granted. I think we should try to learn the truth in this case before telling them anything more. But I do want to ask them a question."

Nancy put in the call to the couple, who were staying in New York City. She told them she had nothing to report, but thought they themselves might get a clue to their missing grandchild through the organization which had sent them to Africa as missionaries. Surely it would have notified Mrs Horton of their capture. "What was the name of the group?" she asked.

Mr Bowen said it was the African Brotherhood Society of New York. "Unfortunately, the Society has been out of existence for several years, so there are no contacts in that direction."

"That's too bad," said Nancy, who realized it would be very difficult to trace anyone who had been in the organization fifteen years before. "Well, I'll say goodbye now. If I learn anything worthwhile, I'll get in touch with you."

George joined the other girls and they discussed the case from every angle. Nancy gave a great sigh. "I think the best thing for me to do right now is clear my brain of the Horton case for a while."

Bess giggled. "How do you propose to do that?"

"By taking a swim. Shall we get ready to go back to the castle? I'd like to find out if anyone is staying there illegally, and if such a person has anything to do with our case."

"Let's go," said George.

Bess was silent. Finally she confessed, "Nancy, while you were telephoning, an absolute dream boy here at the motel asked me to play tennis." She looked off into the distance. "But I'll go with you," she added.

Nancy and George began to laugh. "Like fun you will," said George. "You just can't wait to get out on the court with that boy."

"You know," said Nancy, "it might not be a bad idea. It might fool any inquisitive people if Bess doesn't act as if she were at Long View just as a detective. You go ahead, Bess, and play tennis. If George and I aren't back in three hours, then suppose you and what's-his-name come after us."

Bess blinked and flung up her head. "Okay, but his name's Alan Ryder!" she retorted.

George sniffed. "Better be sure, dear coz, that he is not one of the Seaman gang!"

Bess stamped her foot furiously. "George Fayne, there are times when I could pull your hair right out by the roots!" She stalked off.

Giggling, Nancy and George went to their room. They undressed, put on swim suits, and over them their shorts and shirts. They rolled towels in waterproof bags which they would carry across the moat.

The two girls drove off, excited by the prospect of what they might learn about the old castle. Just before reaching the drawbridge, George began to laugh. "Nancy, maybe you and I are a couple of idiots."

"We probably are," Nancy admitted, "but what put that idea into your head?"

George explained she had heard that in olden times some drawbridges were built so that they could be controlled from the far side of the moat as well as the inside of the castle. "If an unwanted visitor or enemy approached the bridge while it was down, a secret mechanism under the road worked automatically to raise the bridge. Maybe there's hidden machinery on this side. In that case, maybe nobody was at the castle when we walked towards the bridge. We may have set off the mechanism, and up went the bridge!"

"I suppose you could be right," Nancy agreed, "but I still think somebody on the inside let down those two great chains on the bridge. And perhaps the same person was responsible for running water into the moat."

"Well, the bridge is still up, so we're in for a swim," George announced.

Nancy suggested that first they walk along the edge

of the moat to see if they could find the source of the water supply. "It's probably the river, since the far side of the castle faces it."

The girls left their shirts and shorts in the car, then walked around the edge of the moat. They discovered a newly dug trench from Deep River.

"Now I'm sure someone intends to keep out all visitors," Nancy remarked. She grinned. "But not two people named George Fayne and Nancy Drew!"

"Where shall we swim across?" George asked.

Nancy surveyed the area, and decided that a spot a short distance from the drawbridge might be the best place. They walked back.

The two girls put their sandals into the waterproof bags, slipped into the water, and quickly swam to the other side. They pulled themselves up from the moat on to a narrow path and ran to an opening in the stone-walled enclosure, where they thought they could avoid detection while drying off. The place had evidently once been a beautiful garden. There were still pretty flowers among the high weeds and grass.

Suddenly the still air was racked with the sepulchral tones of a man's voice. Slowly but distinctly he warned, "Swim-m-m ba--a-a-ack! Death awaits you here!"

·7·

The Reckless Pilot

THE ominous warning was not repeated. Nancy and George had stopped dead in their tracks. They could see no one.

"Did that man's voice come from inside or outside the castle?" George asked.

"I honestly don't know," Nancy responded. "If we go carefully, do you mind investigating the inside?"

"I'm game," said George. "But *why* didn't we bring flashlights?"

The two girls entered an arched doorway which led to the cellar of the stone castle. Ahead of them was a long corridor with rooms opening off each side. Cobwebs festooned the place. Nancy suggested that George keep looking back and into the rooms on the left. She herself would gaze ahead and glance into the openings on the right.

"This is really spooky," said George. "It looks like an old-time dungeon."

The two sleuths walked as far as there was light to see, but the corridor grew increasingly dimmer as they penetrated into the interior. Most of the rooms had no windows; others had small barred openings high on the outer sides.

Apparently all the rooms were empty with the exception of what once was probably the kitchen. In it was a huge fireplace and a wooden table covered with mould and a few rusty iron kettles.

"This certainly would be a wonderful hiding place," George remarked. "Nancy, I don't want to seem like a loser, but I don't think we should go any farther without a light to guide us."

Nancy agreed. She, too, had begun to feel wary of the dank place.

The two girls returned to the walled garden. Just as they reached it, they heard a car outside the castle. They darted from the enclosure and were just in time to glimpse a saloon disappearing on the far side of the moat. The drawbridge was up. Had it been down and had the car gone across it while they were in the cellar? Or had the car merely come as far as the moat and turned back?

"That car looks like the one Mr Seaman went off in that night I followed him!" George exclaimed. "And the glimpse I had of the driver—well, he could be Mr Seaman himself!"

"Maybe he gave that warning cry," said Nancy.

She suggested that the girls walk round to the front of the castle and try to determine whether or not the car had been parked by the wall.

The girls hurried forward and in a few moments Nancy said excitedly, "Look at these tyre prints, George! They're a real clue to the car that was here."

She pointed to the narrow unpaved road which ran in front of the wall. The tread marks were very distinct. Three of them were exactly alike—their tyres had parallel lines on them.

"But look at this right back one," Nancy said. "The tyre marks are diamond-shaped."

George grinned. "I suppose our next job will be to walk up and down the streets of Deep River and find the car."

"All right," said Nancy. "Tease me all you like, but I think that would be an excellent idea."

She proposed that while the girls were there, they try to find out how the drawbridge worked. The great panelled doorway which it formed was tight in place.

"But how are we going to get behind that wall to find out how the bridge works?" George queried.

"Maybe I could squeeze through that little opening up there," Nancy said, pointing.

Ten feet above them in the sheer rock wall was a rectangular hole through which an ancient cannon was supposed to protrude. Nancy stood on George's shoulders and looked through. Inside, a great courtyard surrounded the castle. The front of the castle was only a sheer wall, but the other three sides had wide stone porticos from which rooms and corridors opened.

The drawbridge, which was in the front wall, Nancy noted, was manipulated by two heavy chains. Someone had to be inside the castle wall to pull them down or release them.

The young sleuth found that she could wriggle through the opening and knew she could drop to the other side. Did she dare?

"I'm going to try it!" Nancy determined.

She disappeared, while George held her breath. If

something happened to Nancy, how could she ever help her? Suddenly she heard the chain begin to rasp and the drawbridge slowly lowered. In a few seconds George was relieved to see Nancy on the other side, unharmed.

With a deep sigh she said, "You found how to work the bridge. Wonderful!"

"The question is, can we get across before somebody pulls it up again?" Nancy speculated.

The two girls sped across the bridge as if a tidal wave were about to overtake them. They reached the other side without anything happening.

"Now let's walk back along the road and see if there's any truth to my theory," said George, "that when a person goes over a certain section of road while the bridge is down, it automatically lifts up."

"Wait!" Nancy called. "Just in case you're right and we want to come here again without swimming across the moat, why don't we try to fasten this end of the bridge down?"

"That's a good idea," George agreed. "Suppose I pile up some rocks, while you go to the car and see if you can find any wire."

By the time Nancy returned, George had lugged several heavy rocks and placed them on either side of the end of the drawbridge.

"That's great!" said Nancy. "I found this wire. Do you suppose we can attach it?"

"There are some posts in the ground with iron hooks on the end of each one," George replied, "I'll bet they were used for this very purpose."

She and Nancy also found stout hooks under the edge

of the drawbridge. Together, the girls fastened several strands of the wire to the hooks, securing the bridge tightly.

Suddenly George began to laugh. "When the person who controls this bridge comes to raise it, can't you see the look on his face? We'd better get out of here before he discovers us!"

"He may have seen us already," said Nancy.

The girls hurried off to the car. They had just started to drive away when Nancy's conscience began to bother her. "You know, George, you and I have been tampering with private property. We could get into trouble over this."

"Don't be silly!" George scoffed. "If we can solve a mystery and catch some crooks, even the police would praise us for finding a way to trap them."

"Aren't you assuming a lot?" Nancy asked. "We don't know if there are any crooks at the castle. That person who warned us away may just be eccentric."

"All the same, I'll bet the owner doesn't know he's staying there and would thank us for finding it out," George defended herself. "And how about Mr Seaman's being here, his wanting to give you something and the moonstone sent to you? Maybe all these have some connection with Moonstone Castle."

Nancy nodded. "Could be."

She said she would leave the bridge wired down, hoping no one would raise it. "If your hunch about the castle being used as a secret headquarters is right, then we should get help and really investigate the place."

"You mean the police?" George asked.

"I was just thinking," Nancy replied, "that instead

of contacting the police, we might try to get Ned and Burt and Dave to go with us."

Burt Eddleton and Dave Evans were college friends of Ned, now camp counsellors at Sylvan Lake near River Heights. Dave dated Bess, and Burt enjoyed taking George to parties.

"Great," said George. "And if the bridge is up and we can't get to the castle by car, we'll hire a boat."

When Bess heard the story of the girls' adventure and Nancy's suggestion, she smiled but said, "You certainly took a chance, Nancy. I'm glad you didn't go any further. As for asking the boys to go sleuthing with us, I'm all for it—a lot more fun than taking the police!"

Nancy put in a call to Ned, who was delighted to hear from her. "I haven't had a letter in ages," he complained. "But this is even better."

Quickly Nancy told of her idea and said that Bess and George were keen about it. "Can you come?"

"Well, speaking for myself, try to keep me away!" Ned replied. "Hold the phone and I'll ask Burt and Dave. We all have a weekend off coming." He came back in a few minutes and said that the boys had accepted the invitation with alacrity and the three would arrive at Long View late the following afternoon.

Bess, when told of the arrangements, said, her dimples showing, "It's a good thing Alan is leaving tomorrow. I hate complications!"

She insisted that the other girls meet Alan, so they walked over to the swimming pool where she had left him a short time before. She introduced Alan, a tanned, good-looking boy. After a few moments' conversation, he said: "I'd like to invite all you girls to a picnic this evening. It's my grandmother's birthday. She lives here in Deep River. That's why my family came up. There are so many of us we can't stay at her house. On Grandmother's birthday the whole family gathers to celebrate it."

Alan explained that the outdoor picnic was to be held at his grandmother's house and gave the girls the address. "Tonight's the big night," he said. "Will you three come and help us pay homage?"

At first the girls demurred, saying that they were total strangers to Mrs Ryder, but Alan was insistent. "The more people who come, the better she likes it. Half the town will be there."

Finally the girls accepted. Nancy said she would drive her own car so the girls would be free to leave without taking Alan away from the celebration.

"But I would like to come for Bess," he said, and she quickly accepted.

All the girls went swimming, then dressed for the picnic. When they were ready to leave, Nancy said, "Bess, we'll follow you and Alan since we don't know the way."

When Alan arrived, they all went over to the car park. Nancy had left the convertible near some rhododendron bushes, but to her surprise, it was not there. She glanced at all the cars in the parking area. Hers was not among them.

"My car's gone!" she cried out.

"What! Why, Nancy, you left it right here not two hours ago!" George exclaimed.

"Someone has stolen it!" Bess said fearfully.

Nancy hurried back inside the motel and phoned police headquarters. She gave a description of the car and the licence number to the sergeant on duty. He said he would send out a radio alarm at once.

"And will you do something else for me?" Nancy asked. "I'd like to know who the owner is of the car with the following licence number." She gave the one George had seen on the saloon car in which Mr Seaman had driven off.

Alan said he felt very sorry for Nancy and would like to help. "We're early for the picnic. Suppose I drive you around town to see if we can spot your car. Maybe it wasn't really stolen—just borrowed."

"I don't think so," said Nancy. "I didn't leave the keys in the ignition and only a car thief would have taken it."

Although the young people drove all over Deep River, they failed to find any trace of the missing convertible. When they finally stopped at police headquarters, Nancy was told that there was no report yet on her car.

"But someone," said the sergeant, "saw a convertible like yours being driven out of town by a woman."

As Nancy pondered this startling information, the sergeant said, "By the way, the owner of the car you asked about is Ralph Seaman. He lives at 24 Willow Road."

"Thank you very much," said Nancy.

By this time Nancy had lost all her enthusiasm for Grandmother Ryder's picnic. But she did not want to seem like a poor sport and accompanied the others. They congratulated the attractive, elderly woman and thanked her for letting them come. Then the young people moved away.

"Did you ever see so much food in your life?" asked Bess as she stared at several long tables filled with all kinds of tasty dishes.

"I'd call this a banquet!" George declared.

Alan and the girls wandered over to it. He handed a plate to each of them from a huge stack at the end of one table and motioned for them to select food. As Nancy was about to put a spoonful of chicken salad on to her plate, someone tapped her arm and she turned.

"Mr Wheeler!" she said. "How do you do?"

"May I speak to you privately for a minute, Miss Drew?" he asked.

Nancy handed her plate to Bess, requesting her to fill it, then walked off with the lawyer.

"I promise not to keep you long," said Mr Wheeler. "You know you've set me thinking about the Horton case."

Mr Wheeler said he had been doing a good bit of reminiscing. He had begun to wonder about the whole thing himself.

· "Something that occurred years ago was recalled to my mind," he said. "I'd like you to go with me to call on a man across the river. I believe he might shed some light on the mystery."

Nancy hesitated, then said, "When do you want to go?"

"As soon as we can get away from this party," the lawyer replied.

"How will we go?" Nancy asked.

"I have a motorboat. It's moored not far from here."

"I'll bring one of my friends with me," said Nancy. "Suppose I meet you over by the musicians." She had just noticed them coming in and taking their places near a lovely rose garden.

"All right. Nine o'clock."

Nancy joined her friends and whispered her plans to Bess and George. Bess said she would like to stay with Alan—it might be best not to tell him about the mystery. George eagerly offered to go.

Promptly at nine o'clock the two girls met Mr Wheeler, who led the way down a path and along the waterfront to a boathouse. He unlocked the entrance door and they all climbed into a sleek motorboat. Mr Wheeler leaned towards the wall, pressed a button, and the big front door rolled up. The lawyer turned on the engine and whizzed from the boathouse.

"He's a fast pilot!" George whispered to Nancy as the boat raced across the river.

They reached the other side and Mr Wheeler spun the wheel, turning the boat sharply to starboard. The girls looked at each other. Although they did not know the river, both felt that in the dark they were much too close to shore for safety.

Mr Wheeler put on more power. George whispered, "For an old man, he's a speed demon!"

Nancy was frightened. She was just about to ask the lawyer to go farther out from the shore when there was a terrific crash. The boat spun round and its passengers were knocked helter-skelter!

· 8 ·

The Canoeist's Clue

It was a full half-minute before Nancy and George collected their wits. They had been badly shaken by the boat crash. Since no other craft was in sight, they assumed their motorboat had hit a rock.

"Nancy!" George cried out. "The boat's filling with water!"

"Yes, and Mr Wheeler's unconscious!"

The girls realized it was futile to try to plug the hole in the boat. They must swim to shore and take Mr Wheeler with them. At this part of the river the bank was very dark. It was tree-lined and impossible for the girls to tell how deep the water was.

Before going over the side, they tried to revive Mr Wheeler. It was hopeless. By this time the water on the floor of the tilted motorboat was six inches deep.

"I'll see how far it is to the bottom here," Nancy offered. She eased herself into the water and disappeared. When she surfaced, she said, "It's over our heads. George, see if there's a flashlight in the boat's compartment."

George yanked open the door. "Yes, there is," she replied.

Nancy asked George if she would please hold it and light the way to shore. She would support Mr Wheeler.

"Can you ease him over the side and lay him on his back?" Nancy asked.

"I'll try." George soon had him in the water.

Nancy tucked one arm around Mr Wheeler's neck to keep him afloat and held him up while she swam with her free arm. George stayed close beside her, holding the strong beam of the flashlight on the bank ahead.

Fortunately, they were close enough to the shore so the swim was not too arduous. They reached it safely and carried the unconscious figure to a flat, open area, where they again tried to revive him. It was useless.

George and Nancy peered into the dark night, hoping to see lights from a house. But neither girl saw any.

"I guess we'll have to yell for help!' Nancy said.

She began calling, but there was no response. George took up the cry, and the two friends thought their shouts would surely rouse Mr Wheeler. But he lay still on the grass.

"I'll SOS with the flashlight," Nancy said finally. "Maybe somebody will pick it up."

She began—three dots, three dashes, followed by three dots. After waiting several seconds the young sleuth repeated the distress signal.

Suddenly the girls heard a hello from the water. "You in trouble?" a man's voice called.

"Yes. Our boat hit a rock. We're here on shore with an injured man."

"I'll be right there," the stranger promised.

Within a few minutes a canoe pulled up to the shore. In it were a couple, who jumped out at once.

The young man went over to Mr Wheeler, got down on one knee, and felt the man's pulse.

Meanwhile, the girl said, "We're Amy Cadmus and Art Munson. Art's a medical student."

"Thank goodness for that," said George, and introduced herself and Nancy.

Art quickly examined Mr Wheeler, then said, "We must get this man to the Deep River Hospital immediately."

"Is there a road near here?" Nancy asked.

"No, there isn't. This area is almost a wilderness. I'll be glad to take the man to the hospital in our canoe. Amy, suppose you come with me. Later, I'll return for you girls. For Pete's sake, you're shivering."

"Well, we're soaking wet," George said. "And of course Mr Wheeler is, too."

"He's John Wheeler, a retired lawyer of Deep River," said Nancy.

"Oh, really?" said Amy. "I know him."

In Art's well-equipped canoe were two raincoats and a large tarpaulin. He handed a raincoat to each of the soaking-wet girls. Mr Wheeler was laid in the canoe and the tarpaulin placed over him.

The canoeists paddled off, making fast time across the river. Nevertheless, for Nancy and George the wait seemed interminable. At last, however, Art reappeared.

As Nancy and George climbed into the canoe, Art said, "I called an ambulance as soon as we reached the other side. Amy said she would stay there and tell the doctor what happened and who Mr Wheeler is."

"Do you think he's going to be all right?" Nancy asked.

"It's hard to say," the young medical student replied. "He hadn't regained consciousness when I left him."

George offered to take the extra paddle and it was not long before they reached town. Amy was waiting for them on the dock. She said the ambulance had come and gone. Mr Wheeler was still unconscious.

"Where are you girls staying?" she asked.

"At the Long View Motel," Nancy replied.

Art said he had a car nearby and offered to drive the girls home. Grinning, he added, "Doctor Munson orders hot baths and a good night's sleep."

Nancy and George laughed and said they would certainly obey his orders.

As they headed for the motel, Amy said to George, "How do you happen to have a boy's name, or isn't George your real name?"

George smiled. "It's my real name all right. According to the story, my parents were so sure I was going to be a boy, they had picked out only the name George, so they decided to give it to me, anyway."

"I like it," said Amy. "Unusual names intrigue me. My sister, who is eighteen, has a friend whose name I love. It's Jodine."

"That is unusual," Nancy agreed. "Is she called that?"

"No, which I think is a shame. She's called Jody." Amy went on to say that Jody was a wonderful girl. "I wish you could meet her while you're here. Her last name is Armstrong and she lives on Birchwood Lane—that's the street alongside the high school. She has had the name Armstrong only since she was about three or four years old, when she was adopted."

Nancy and George, interested at once, glanced at each other. Had they picked up a clue to Joanie Horton? Trying to sound nonchalant, Nancy asked, "Was Jody adopted here in Deep River?"

"Her present parents got her from an adoption society in the next town, I believe."

"I'd love to meet her," said Nancy. "While we're here, could you introduce us?"

Amy said unfortunately both she and her sister were going out of town early the next morning on holiday. "But Jody would love to meet you just the same. Tell her you saw me and that I suggested you girls get together."

Nancy was delighted with the information. She would certainly look up Jody Armstrong!

By this time the car had reached the motel. Nancy and George thanked Art and Amy for their kindness in taking care of Mr Wheeler and for rescuing them.

"I'm sorry we won't see you again," said Nancy. "Have a marvellous time on your holiday."

"I'm sure we will," said Amy. "Too bad that Art won't be here. This is the last day of his vacation. He's going back to medical school in New York City tomorrow."

Nancy and George returned the raincoats to their kind donors, then walked into the motel reception.

Bess Marvin ran towards them. "My goodness, what happened to you? You're all wet!"

Mrs Thompson, who had risen from a chair, now reached the bedraggled girls. "Bess and I have been dreadfully worried about you."

Quickly Nancy and George told what had happened.

Mrs Thompson insisted that they follow Art Munson's advice. "As soon as you're in bed, I'll bring you some hot cocoa and biscuits."

"It would taste mighty good, I admit," said Nancy.

Bess offered to help Mrs Thompson and went to her private kitchen. When the cocoa and biscuits were ready, Bess carried them to the girls' room. While Nancy and George sat up in bed, sipping the hot, soothing cocoa, they told Bess about Jody Armstrong.

At once Bess had the same thought as Nancy and George. "Do you think Jody Armstrong is really Joanie Horton?" she asked excitedly.

"Let's go to see her tomorrow!" Nancy said.

The Vanishing Patient

EXCITED by the sleuthing ahead of them, Nancy, Bess, and George got up early the following morning. Since the weather forecast predicted a hot day, the girls put on lightweight cotton dresses.

"I wish I felt as cool as I look," said Bess, staring at herself in the mirror. "I think we're hot on the trail of something and it makes me even hotter to think about it!"

Nancy and Bess laughed, and George remarked, "I hope the only cooling-off swim I have today will not be in the moat but in the *mot*-el pool!"

Bess's reaction to the pun was to throw a pillow at her cousin. Still laughing, Nancy went to the motel reception and phoned for a taxi to take them to the same restaurant for breakfast. When they finished eating, Nancy said she wanted to make two phone calls—one to the hospital and the other to police headquarters.

"To find out about Mr Wheeler and about your car?" Bess asked. Nancy nodded.

The hospital lines were engaged, so Nancy phoned police headquarters. She learned that there was no word yet of her car. With a sigh she again dialled the hospital, only to get an engaged tone.

"I'll call in there later," the young sleuth decided

She came back to her friends and reported her findings. Then she said, "It's rather early to call on the Armstrongs. I have a suggestion. Let's find out how far it is to Willow Road. We might walk there, instead of calling a taxi, and take a look at Mr Seaman's house."

"Why don't we visit him?" George suggested.

"Let's decide what to do when we get there."

Nancy found out from the waitress that Willow Road was only about half a mile away. The girls decided to walk. They set out at a brisk pace.

On the way Bess brought up the subject of Nancy's mysterious gift of a moonstone. "Do you realize we have never had one single clue to explain that?"

"I know," said Nancy. "But I feel that sooner or later the donor is going to give himself or herself away."

George began to tease Nancy once more about the mysterious person being an admirer. She said, "Wait until Ned gets here. You probably can trap him into confessing."

Nancy was spared the necessity of a retort because Bess called out, "This is Willow Road."

The girls turned into the street and presently reached the address given to Nancy by the police. Number twenty-four gave every evidence of being deserted. Grass, weeds, and unkempt flowers were tall. Two small chairs on the porch lay upside down as if the wind had blown them over.

"I'm sure no one is living here," she said, "but we'll ring the bell, anyway."

She pushed the button and also clapped the knocker, but there was no response.

"This sure complicates our case," said George.

"I wonder," Nancy mused, "whether it was just a phoney address Mr Seaman used, knowing the house was vacant, or whether he's staying away from it for some particular reason."

"Oh, let's forget him," Bess suggested. "I'm more interested in what we're going to find out about Jody Armstrong."

It was a mile to the Armstrong home, but by walking it, the girls arrived there at a reasonable hour for visiting.

As they went up the front path, Nancy whispered to the cousins, "We'll have to be careful not to mention the subject of Jody and the adoption. Her parents may be touchy about it and not want to know who Jody's real parents might have been. Let's hope Mrs Armstrong brings up the matter."

"You're right," said Bess. "Let's not give any hint as to what we're trying to find out."

"I have the picture of Joanie Horton in my bag," said Nancy. "If we can only see a picture of Jody taken soon after the Armstrongs adopted her, perhaps we could compare the two in private."

Hopefully the three girls went to the door and Nancy rang the bell. A pleasant attractive woman of about forty answered. She smiled at the callers. "Mrs Armstrong?" Nancy inquired.

"Yes."

Nancy told of having met Amy Cadmus and Amy's suggestion that the girls get in touch with Jody. "We're staying at a motel and don't know anyone in town."

"Do come in," Mrs Armstrong invited the callers.

"I'm sorry Jody isn't here. She went with her father on a business trip and won't be home until this evening.'

Nancy smiled. "We'll have to see your daughter another time then," she said.

"Please don't go," Mrs Armstrong said cordially. "I'm going to be lonely here by myself all day. I'd love to talk to you. Tell me how you happened to come to Deep River."

At once Bess spoke up. "Mother knew about the darling motel here."

"It *is* a very attractive place," Mrs Armstrong agreed.

After a little while, Nancy remarked, "Jodine is a lovely but rather unusual name."

"Yes, it is," Mrs Armstrong agreed. She looked into space for a few seconds, then added, "Mr Armstrong and I didn't give it to her. We adopted our daughter and that was the name she had."

"Have you always called her Jody?" Bess asked.

Mrs Armstrong said that the nickname too had already been given to their daughter, apparently by her own mother. "The adoption took place many years ago. There's no secret to the story—people around here know it. Jody herself has been told what happened, but I doubt that she ever thinks about it. We love her very much and we're her parents now."

Mrs Armstrong revealed that when Jody was about three years of age, she was left at the adoption society in the town next to Deep River. "Mr Armstrong and I had asked for a child, and when Jody was offered to us, we both fell in love with her. She had been found asleep in the lounge of the society. There was a note pinned to her dress which said that she was Jodine Holt, and her nickname was Jody. Scrawled on the papers were the words, 'I am giving up all rights to this child and offer her for adoption. Her mother.' "

There was a somewhat awkward pause, then Nancy, smiling, said, "But everything has turned out wonderfully for her."

"We hope so. Jody has always been an adorable child. That's her picture on the piano."

The three girls got up to look at the photograph of a tall, slender, attractive, dark-haired girl.

"She's lovely!" Bess exclaimed. As Nancy and George added their compliments, Mrs Armstrong beamed delightedly.

"She photographs so well," said Nancy, "you must have taken lots of pictures of her." She hoped fervently that Mrs Armstrong would bring out some of them.

"Oh, yes, indeed," the woman said. "But as the years go on, the older pictures somehow get up to the attic and are packed away."

Nancy felt that the girls had stayed long enough. She merely remarked that she was more eager than ever to meet Jody and asked that the girl get in touch with her as soon as it was convenient.

Jody's mother promised to give her the message, then said, "I want my daughter to meet you girls, too."

She accompanied her three visitors to the door and they said goodbye. As they walked up the street arm in arm, Bess asked, "Well, did we learn anything or not?"

"I'm puzzled by that note which was pinned to Jody's dress," said Nancy. "If, by any chance, she *is* Joanie Horton—you will admit there is a great similarity in names—then the little girl probably was kidnapped, and the note was a forgery, since her mother wasn't living. By getting the child out of the way, an impostor was able to claim Mrs Horton's estate."

Nancy went on to say that if this theory were true, the person who had perpetrated the kidnapping and theft had thought out the plan in great detail, even to the name. The little girl had been old enough to say her own name, so a pseudonym had been chosen which was similar.

"You mean," Bess said, "if she gave her name as Joanie Horton, people might think she was mispronouncing Jody Holt?"

Nancy nodded. "I do hope Jody gets in touch with us," she remarked. "If she does, I don't think we should mention adoption to her. Let's see if we can pick up any clues about her childhood, though."

"What are we going to do now?" Bess asked.

"I think our next stop should be the hospital," Nancy replied, "to find out how Mr Wheeler is. I hope he'll be well enough to see us. I want to ask him who the man is that he wanted us to meet."

The girls entered the hospital. There was a great commotion. Nurses and doctors were talking excitedly with two policemen.

Wondering what had happened, Nancy went up to the desk and asked the receptionist on duty if she and her friends might see Mr Wheeler.

"Mr Wheeler!" the woman cried out. "He's the patient who was kidnapped from here this morning!"

Nancy stared in stupefaction, as the receptionist called out to members of the hospital staff, "Here's somebody who knows Mr Wheeler."

At once Nancy was surrounded and plied with questions. She said she knew nothing about what had happened. "I was with Mr Wheeler last night when he had the boat accident."

"Are you the girl who saved his life?" asked one of the doctors.

Nancy blushed. "Well, my friend over there and I did." She beckoned for George to come forward with Bess.

They, too, were stunned to hear that Mr Wheeler was missing from the hospital.

One of the nurses explained. "It happened before visiting hours began," she said. "We have a very ill patient on the first floor where Mr Wheeler was. All the nurses on duty there were in the sick woman's room for a while. We pieced the story together. Apparently a man dressed as an orderly and a woman as a nurse came in, put Mr Wheeler on an operating trolley, and took him by lift to the ground floor. There they must have transferred him to a wheel chair and taken him off by car."

"How dreadful!" Bess exclaimed.

"Didn't he make any protest or outcry?" Nancy queried.

"Mr Wheeler was only semiconscious," the nurse replied. "We had even put the side guards up on his bed so that he would be safe when left alone."

One of the policemen quizzed Nancy and her friends, asking if they could give any clue as to who the abductors might be.

"I'm afraid not," Nancy replied. "We're strangers in town. We're staying at the Long View Motel. Mr

Wheeler attended a party we were at last night and took George and myself out in his boat."

"With a disastrous ending," George added.

Nancy asked permission to speak to any nurses on duty who might have helped to take care of Mr Wheeler. She was told that the only one in the hospital at the moment who had taken care of him was Mrs Straff on the first floor, but Nancy was welcome to go ahead and speak to her.

The nurse was a kindly middle-aged woman. She said she felt perfectly dreadful about the kidnapping and could not understand how it had occurred. "I guess we were all with that sick woman longer than we thought."

"I do hope the authorities will find him soon," said Nancy. "I don't know Mr Wheeler very well. He was taking me across the river to see an acquaintance of his. I didn't learn the person's name and I'm curious to know who he is. Did Mr Wheeler ever talk while he was semiconscious?"

"Oh, yes, he mumbled a great deal," Mrs Straff replied. "I couldn't get much out of it, but maybe the name of the person you're trying to find out about is the one he kept repeating. It was Peter Judd. I've never heard of him."

"He may be the man," said Nancy, and thanked the woman for the information.

The girls left the hospital. When they were on the street once more, Nancy smiled and said, "I'll bet Mrs Hemstead will know who Peter Judd is!"

Bess and George giggled, and the girls turned towards the Brass Kettle.

"We'll have an early lunch," Nancy remarked. "We may see Mrs Hemstead first. Remember, you're to call me Irene."

"Oh, that's right," said Bess. "Lead the way, Miss Irene Insbruck!"

The three friends walked through the door of the tearoom. As usual, Mrs Hemstead was seated in her rocking chair, wearing the same black dress with the ruching collar. The instant she saw the girls, her wrinkled face broke into a great grin.

In her high-pitched voice, she asked, "Well, how are you, Nancy Drew, detective?"

·10·

Peter Judd

WHEN confronted with a startling statement, Nancy usually was able to hide her surprise. This time she did not succeed—Mrs Hemstead's greeting was too astounding.

"So you've found me out," she said, after a moment. "Who told you?"

The old lady wagged her head. "I don't know. An anonymous note came in today's post."

From a deep pocket in her skirt, Mrs Hemstead withdrew the folded piece of paper. She handed the note to Nancy. Bess and George crowded near her to read the message printed on it. The note was short and to the point:

> DON'T BE FOOLED. THE GIRL CALLING HERSELF IRENE INSBRUCK IS REALLY NANCY DREW. SHE'S A DETECTIVE. BE-WARE WHAT YOU SAY TO HER OR YOU MAY GET INTO TROUBLE.

Bess sniffed. "I hate people who write anonymous notes. Why didn't the person who wrote this come right out in the open and tell you?"

"How should I know?" Mrs Hemstead asked in a high complaining voice.

Nancy was sure of one thing—the sender of the note had done it with the express purpose of trying to frighten Mrs Hemstead into revealing no more gossip to Nancy. "But he doesn't stand a chance of succeeding," Nancy told herself with determination.

She sighed and said aloud, "Well, now, I suppose, Mrs Hemstead, that you will tell this secret about my identity to Mr Seaman?"

For once, the old lady did not reply. Perhaps she was a little afraid of the warning in the note. Nancy decided that if the girls were going to learn anything further, she would have to do some bargaining with Mrs Hemstead.

Smiling, she said, "I've just learned something amazing that happened in your town this morning."

Instantly the old lady leaned forward expectantly. "What was it?" she asked eagerly.

The young sleuth laughed. "Oh, I can keep secrets, too."

Mrs Hemstead frowned and rocked back and forth furiously for several seconds. Finally she stopped.

"I don't know whether I'll tell Mr Seaman or not," she said flatly. "I suppose you'd like to know more about him. Well, I can't tell you much more than I already have. He's been coming here for several years— always stops and talks to me to get the local news. I figure he's a travelling salesman."

Nancy did not reveal the fact that he had a Deep River address. Because of Mrs Hemstead's idea that he was from out of town, Nancy was sure now that Mr

Seaman had given a fictitious address when obtainin his driver's licence. Could he have written the warnin, note to Mrs Hemstead? Nancy wondered.

The old lady went on, "The other day when M Seaman came in, he said he was looking for a gir named Nancy Drew who was coming to town. H wanted to find out where she was staying."

"But why?" George put in. "Nancy isn't acquainte with him."

Mrs Hemstead shrugged. "I don't know. Mr Sea man acted as if he wanted to date you, Nancy. Whe you told me your name was Irene, I figured you must b another girl friend." The elderly woman chuckle cheerfully. "I thought to myself, 'Here's a complica tion!' What's this all about, anyway?"

"What do you mean?" Nancy countered.

After another several seconds of furious rocking, Mr Hemstead said, "I mean, here you are, a detective using an assumed name and Mr Seaman asking fo you—"

Nancy laughed. "I suggest that you ask Mr Seaman After all, he inquired about me first."

Before Mrs Hemstead could do any more delving the young sleuth said, "Girls, I'm absolutely starved Let's go and eat!"

She and the cousins escaped into the dining-room and found a table far from the waiting-room door. A they unfolded their napkins, George remarked, "Speak ing of complications, this mystery gets more tangled by the minute."

"I don't like the idea of that anonymous note Nancy," said Bess. "It might mean danger for you!"

Nancy merely smiled. "You and George are my bodyguards. Can't you keep me from the big bad wolves? You know, Mr Seaman might have sent that note."

The cousins nodded worriedly. The three ate a light lunch, then Nancy said, "You know we came to the Brass Kettle in the first place to see if Mrs Hemstead knows Peter Judd. I admit I'd forgotten all about it until this moment."

After the girls had paid their bill, they went back to the waiting-room. Mrs Hemstead was not there and Nancy wondered how soon she would return. George learned from the woman's daughter that she was having her midday meal and a rest in her room upstairs.

"But Mother will be down in a little while," she said. "Would you like to wait?"

Nancy decided to do so. The girls sat down for a few minutes, then got up and began to look at the various articles in the old-fashioned room. Nancy examined the antique map on the wall which designated the local area as Moonstone Valley. Deep River was shown as a place with only a few houses and shops. There were two side streets and at the end of one, at the river, stood a large mill.

"What a picturesque town this must have been!" Nancy thought.

At that moment Mrs Hemstead returned to the room and took her place in the old chair.

"Did you enjoy your lunch?" she asked.

"Yes, indeed," Bess replied. "If I ate here very often, I'd put on pounds and pounds!"

"My daughter has established a good reputation,"

the elderly woman said proudly. "Folks come from miles and miles away."

Nancy asked, "Did you ever hear of a man named Mr Peter Judd?"

"Indeed I have," Mrs Hemstead replied quickly. "Strange old fellow."

"Strange?" Nancy repeated.

"That's what folks say. Peter Judd used to be a train conductor. Now he's retired and lives across the river in a little cottage. Won't have a soul help him—he does all his own cooking and laundry work. Has his place full of railway posters. The dishes and cutlery he uses are all from railway dining cars."

The girls giggled. Encouraged by their interest Mrs Hemstead added, "You couldn't mistake his house. Right on the front lawn he has an enormous bell that was taken from an old-fashioned locomotive. Sometimes boys sneak in there and ring it. You can hear it clear across the river!"

"I'd like to see it," said Nancy. "Just where *is* his house?"

Mrs Hemstead said that if they went directly across the river and turned downstream for a mile, they would come to a jetty with a string of railway carriages painted on the overhang.

"That's his place."

The girls thanked the elderly woman and said goodbye. They went at once to a boat hire service for a small motorboat. Nancy took the wheel and the little craft skimmed across the river. Some distance from shore, she headed downstream, planning to turn in towards Mr Judd's jetty.

On the way, George showed Bess Mr Wheeler's half-submerged motorboat.

Bess shuddered a bit. "You had a narrow escape," she said.

"I wonder when the authorities are going to take the boat away?" George mused. "I'd think it would be a hazard to other boats."

Nancy chuckled. "Not so much as that rock we hit!"

"Nancy, who do you think kidnapped Mr Wheeler?" Bess asked.

The young sleuth had a ready answer. "The same persons who kidnapped Joanie Horton. I think they were afraid Mr Wheeler might reopen the case, bringing a fraud to light. In fact, they may think Dad had asked Mr Wheeler's assistance, even though he is retired."

They found Peter Judd's jetty and moored alongside it. As they walked up an incline to his little white cottage, they saw the retired railway conductor working in his garden near the great engine bell. Nancy spoke to him, admiring the bell and his beautiful roses.

Mr Judd was cordial and invited the girls inside his home. They found it interesting, despite Mrs Hemstead's remarks. And Peter Judd certainly did not seem eccentric!

"How did you happen to know about me?" he asked.

At once Nancy told him about Mr Wheeler, the accident, and the kidnapping.

"What a low-down trick!" Mr Judd cried, incensed. "What do you think is the reason?"

"We can only guess," said Nancy. "Possibly you can help solve the riddle. Do you know why Mr Wheeler was bringing my friend George and me here? He hinted

that it had something to do with the settlement c
Mrs Horton's estate many years ago."

Peter Judd was thoughtful for several seconds, as i
trying to decide whether or not to tell these strange girl
something he knew. Finally he said:

"I believe I do. After that young lady Joan Horto
got all her grandmother's money, she went away—
nobody knew where. Suddenly I remembered some
thing that had happened on my train a little over si:
months before old Mrs Horton died. I went to M
Wheeler and told him about it, but he just laughed a
me. But now I think maybe he has decided there wa
something to it."

Eagerly Nancy asked, "What is the story?"

· 11 ·

The Tower Signaller

NANCY, Bess, and George pulled chairs close to Mr Peter Judd so that they would not miss one word of the story he was about to tell.

Suddenly Nancy jumped up and commanded, "Wait!" She turned and dashed towards the front door, calling as she went, "Girls, run out the back way and stop that man!"

Mr Judd was amazed. He did not know what Nancy meant, but he hurried to a window and looked outside. He was just in time to see Nancy take off at full speed after a man who was fleeing down the embankment towards the dock. Before she could reach him, the man jumped into a motorboat tied alongside the girls' rented boat and roared off.

Nancy came to a full stop on the jetty. It would be useless to try to pursue the man; he had too much of a head start. Bess and George ran up to her.

"Who was he?" Bess asked. "Why were you chasing him?"

The young sleuth explained that as Mr Judd was about to start his story, she had seen the top of the head of an eavesdropper just outside the window. "I got a better look at him as he jumped into his boat. I think he's the man you said followed me in River Heights—the one who was following George here in Deep River. He's the man I said looked familiar."

"He seems determined to find out what we're doing," Bess remarked.

"I'll say he is," George agreed. "So far as I'm concerned, he's definitely an enemy."

"And maybe he's one of the kidnappers," Bess suggested. "Why don't we follow him? He might lead us to Mr Wheeler."

George scoffed at this idea. "That's exactly what he *wouldn't* do," she said, laughing. "Anyhow, we wouldn't be able to overtake him now."

Nancy nodded. "Let's go back and hear Mr Judd's story," she suggested.

Inside the cottage once more, she described the eavesdropper and their past encounters with him. "Have you any idea who he might be?"

Mr Judd shook his head, and Nancy begged him to tell the story which had been interrupted.

"While I was on a train running direct from New York City to Deep River some fifteen years ago," he began, "I specially noted three passengers in one of the carriages—a man, a woman, and a very pretty little girl between two and three years old. When I had some free time I stopped to talk to her. She said her name was Joanie and she was going to stay with her other granny."

Nancy, Bess, and George listened intently. This was indeed interesting!

"Joanie made a remark that I have never forgotten. She said her grandaddy and grandmummy she was with were going far away to tell people about God."

"Missionaries?" Bess queried.

"I suppose so," said Mr Judd. "Well, the little girl and her grandparents got off in Deep River and I never saw any of them again. Months later, when I heard about Mrs Horton and her grown-up granddaughter named Joanie, I remembered about those folks on the train. I kept thinking about that grown-up girl getting all the money and thought I ought to tell Mr Wheeler the story."

George blurted out, "You told this to Mr Wheeler all that time ago and he didn't do anything about it?"

"As I said before, he just laughed at me. I felt kind of silly and never mentioned the story again to anyone. Now, maybe, Mr Wheeler has changed his mind and wants to hear about it in more detail."

"No doubt," Nancy agreed. "Can you give us the details?"

"The little girl had big, blue eyes and blond curls."

Nancy excitedly opened her bag and took out the picture of young Joanie Horton at the age of two. "Is this the child?" she asked.

It was now Mr Judd's turn to look astounded. "It certainly looks like her," the ex-conductor said. "Of course it was a long time ago, but this is just about the way I remember little Joanie."

Mr Judd asked Nancy to explain her connection with the Horton family. "Actually, it's my father's case," she replied, knowing that it might be unwise to reveal her part in the investigation. "I expect my dad to come to Deep River in a little while. He'll probably come to call on you very soon."

This evasive answer seemed to satisfy Mr Judd, and

before he had a chance to say anything more, Nancy got up, thanked him, and said the girls must leave.

"I certainly hope they find Mr Wheeler soon," Mr Judd called, as his visitors went towards the jetty.

When the girls were seated in their boat, Nancy's face wore a broad grin. "This is the best clue yet!" she exclaimed.

"It's simply marvellous!" said Bess. "How are you going to develop it?"

Nancy said she thought it might be a good idea to do a little sleuthing among the shopkeepers in town. "There may be some who were here fifteen years ago, and perhaps could tell us if any articles for a small child were sent out to the Horton home." Nancy suggested that the girls divide up the shopping area and make separate calls on the shopkeepers.

This bit of delving took until the latter part of the afternoon. They had about given up hope of any further clue, until Nancy entered a small toy shop. It was run by an elderly man and woman. After learning that the couple had been in town for over thirty years, Nancy asked her question.

The man and woman looked at each other, then smiled. Finally the woman said, "I remember something about a child's gift very well. The most beautiful doll and carriage we have ever sold were ordered over the telephone at Christmas time and delivered to the Horton home."

"Did the person who delivered it see a little girl there?" Nancy asked.

"No. Our messenger saw no one. I remember clearly how he reported to us that a cheque and a note had been left on the Horton porch with instructions for him to leave the toys there."

The man shopkeeper, curious, asked Nancy why she had made her inquiry. As nonchalantly as possible, Nancy answered, "My father is interested in the Horton family. My friends and I came up here on holiday and he asked me to find out what I could about them."

"I see," said the man. "Can't tell you anything more." He turned and walked into a back room. At the same time, a boy came in through the front door and the woman went to serve him. The girls left.

"This is our day for good luck," said Bess. "Maybe the moonstone is bringing it!"

Nancy laughed, but agreed that they had picked up two valuable clues. "Right now I have so many trails to follow, I don't know which to take. The one I'd like most to pursue would be the opportunity of talking to Jody Armstrong."

"Then why don't you?" said George. "She's probably home by now."

"No," said Nancy. "If I seem like a friendship pusher, the Armstrongs may become suspicious and not let me see Jody at all."

"You're right," said Bess. "Anyhow, don't forget, the boys are coming today. I want to shampoo my hair before they get here—it's a mess after all our trekking around and the wind blowing it in that boat."

The girls took a taxi to the motel. As soon as they reached it, Nancy went to the telephone. She called police headquarters and asked if there was any news of her stolen car.

"Not a trace," said the officer on duty. "I'm sorry, Miss Drew. We're still working hard trying to find it."

Nancy next asked whether Mr Wheeler had been found. Again the answer was no. Nancy hung up.

In spite of this disappointment and worry over the whereabouts of the injured lawyer, the day's new clues spurred Nancy on. She felt too excited to go to her room to rest or start dressing. "I think I'll get the binoculars and take another look at that castle," she decided.

She got the glasses and went out to the terrace. As she trained the binoculars on the distant building, the tower of the castle came into sharp focus.

Nancy gasped. A man, bearded and unkempt, stood on the roof of the tower. He, too, held glasses to his eyes. They were trained directly on the motel and Nancy!

Instantly Nancy dodged behind a tree. "I hope he didn't see me." Though out of sight, she continued to focus her own binoculars on him.

The man put down his binoculars and began to make strange motions with his hands. Nancy watched him intently.

She asked herself, "Has that man gone crazy or is he trying to signal someone?"

· 12 ·

Impending Crash

"Hi, SLEUTH!" a male voice called.

She lowered the binoculars and turned quickly. "Ned!" she cried out.

He kissed her, then asked how she was making out with her mystery case. In answer, Nancy handed him the binoculars and pointed towards the tower of the castle. "See if you can figure out what that man is doing," she suggested.

Ned adjusted the glasses. Finally he said, frowning, "With that long beard and wild hair the fellow looks like some kind of a nut. But actually I think he's doing his own version of semaphore. Maybe he's sending a message in code."

Nancy took the glasses again and watched the strange man. He continued the same motions for another half minute, then disappeared.

"I guess he's gone inside the castle," she said.

Ned took the binoculars. "Suppose I watch to see if he comes outside the castle, and if so, where he goes and what he does. Meanwhile, you bring me up to date on the news."

Nancy told him about the missing Joanie Horton, and her suspicion that Mrs Horton's servants were connected with the child's disappearance. She outlined Mr Wheeler's part in settling the Horton estate, his disappearance from the hospital, Peter Judd's story and the mysterious men who had followed her and George.

"One of them calls himself Mr Seaman."

"So you suspect some great hoax was perpetrated fourteen years ago," Ned commented. "I'd say this is a big order for us boys to deliver over a weekend, but we'll do our best."

Though Ned and Nancy waited for some time, with the glasses trained on the castle, no one appeared either on the tower or the grounds. Ned grinned. "I guess that strange fellow lives there," he said. "Not too bad a place if you don't have to pay rent."

"He's probably the person who warned George and me away from the castle when we swam over to it," Nancy said.

"In that case, you girls shouldn't go there alone again."

Nancy and Ned walked to the motel, discussing the tower signaller and wondering to whom he was sending a message. "It may or may not have anything to do with the case I'm trying to solve," Nancy remarked.

"If it has," said Ned, "the receiver might be Mr Seaman or that other man."

Nancy nodded and led the way into the motel reception office where they found Bess and George talking excitedly with Dave Evans and Burt Eddleton. She introduced Ned to Mrs Thompson, who in turn showed him the room where the three boys would sleep.

Forty minutes later the young people, in attractive

suits and dresses, met in reception and discussed where to have dinner. Mrs Thompson suggested a popular dining spot. "They have dancing and the music is really excellent."

"That's the place for me," said Dave, taking a few dance steps.

Nancy and her friends decided to try the spot and set off in Ned's car.

"No leads on your convertible?" he asked Nancy, who sat in front beside him.

"Not one! We hike and taxi. But getting to the castle hasn't been on our schedule. Let's go right after church tomorrow."

"I'm at your service," said Ned.

The restaurant building proved to be a large, modern concrete structure with geometric designs painted on it in flamboyant colours. The interior decor was ultra-fashionable and a group was already playing a well-known tune.

"It looks like a sophisticated place in New York City!" Ned remarked in surprise.

Bess tossed her head. "What makes you think Moonstone Valley isn't up to date?"

The three boys were puzzled and Dave asked, "Moonstone Valley?"

"Oh, somebody changed its name," Bess explained. "It's now called Deep River Valley, but I think Moonstone is much more romantic."

After the three couples were seated at a table, Bess continued, "Speaking of moonstones, did you know Nancy received a beautiful one as a gift?" Bess looked directly at Ned Nickerson.

"No, she didn't tell me," he answered. There was nothing in the way he said it to indicate that he was the donor.

"It's very mysterious," Bess went on. "There wasn't any card with the gift—just a warning note."

"A warning?" Ned repeated. "What kind?"

Bess declared that she would not tell him another word until he confessed he had played the joke. Ned denied this vigorously. "Honestly, I didn't send the moonstone," he declared. "But I'd certainly like to know who did. Tell me about this warning."

The whole story was told and the boys agreed it was mysterious. None of them thought it was funny; rather, something to be taken quite seriously.

"I suppose you figure there's some connection between your moonstone and Moonstone Valley," Burt said.

"If there is, it eludes me completely," Nancy answered. "But if the sender had a joke in mind or a warning, why didn't he send a cheap stone? This is one of the most beautiful moonstones I've ever seen. I'll show it to you." She took it from her evening bag.

"Wow! What a gift!" Burt exclaimed.

As a waiter came to their table, the three couples turned their attention to dinner and dancing. They spent several hours at the attractive restaurant, then left.

"It's too early to go directly home," said Ned. "How about hiring a motorboat if we can and taking a cruise on the river?"

Bess looked up at the sky. "What a beautiful moon!"

he exclaimed. "It would be absolutely heavenly on the water. Let's do it!"

Nancy directed Ned to a jetty where she thought boats could be hired at night. They found one that gave twenty-four-hour service. Ned parked and went inside to make inquiries. Presently he returned and said they would take a sleek motorboat named the *Water Witch*.

"*Which* water?" Dave punned, whereupon Burt pretended to throw him into the river.

The six young people climbed in and Ned took the wheel.

"If you want to see Mr Wheeler's wrecked boat, it's across the river and down a short distance," said Nancy.

Ned followed her directions and had just turned downstream when they all became aware of a motorboat coming towards them. It was headed directly for their boat.

At once Ned turned his craft. The approaching boat still came at them, as if drawn by a magnet. Ned sounded his horn. The other pilot paid no attention.

"Is that fellow loco?" Burt asked worriedly.

Ned dodged this way and that to get out of the path of the oncoming craft.

"It's going to hit us!" Bess screamed.

Just before the strange boat reached them, its pilot dived into the water. Ned swerved in a desperate attempt to avoid both the motorboat and the swimmer. His effort was successful.

"Good work!" said George.

Everyone looked to see what had become of the pilot who had jumped overboard.

"I see him!" Nancy cried out. "He's swimmin
towards the shore."

"I guess he's safe," said Ned. "Now we'd better chas
that boat and try to stop it before it does any damage!"

The race was on. Ned gave his own craft full powe
and little by little inched up on the pilotless boat.

"I'll jump across," Burt offered, and made a flyin
leap. He took the wheel, which he found responde
well. "There's nothing the matter with this steerin
mechanism. That fellow intended to hit us for sure!"
He invited George to hop in beside him and asked
"Now where do we go?"

"I suppose we should take the boat back with us t
the jetty and explain what happened," said Nancy.

"But I'd like to see that castle first," said Ned. "I
that the building over there?"

"Yes."

The two boats headed for the rickety jetty, which
evidently had been used by the former tenants of th
castle.

Suddenly Nancy exclaimed, "I saw a light moving i
the castle!"

"I did too," Ned agreed.

"That bearded man must be there!" Bess suggested

George gave a great sigh. "There's one way to find
out. Why don't we tie up here and you boys car
investigate?"

She was just about to get out of the stranger's speed
boat when the group heard a shrill whistle. They turned
Coming at a fast clip was a police launch. A larg
searchlight pinpointed the *Water Witch* and the othe
craft.

The young people in both boats stayed in their seats. In a few seconds the launch pulled up alongside and stopped.

The chief officer leaned over the railing and said, "So you're the ones who stole the boat!"

Nancy and her friends were dumfounded. She protested firmly that they had not stolen the boat and told exactly what had happened.

"Sorry, miss, but that sounds as if you're just trying to shift the blame on to somebody else."

"It's the truth!" Nancy insisted, and the others backed up her story.

"Well, you can tell them down at headquarters," the officer said. To Burt and George he added, "Get out and come aboard the launch."

Angry but obedient, the pair climbed into the police launch. Another officer jumped aboard the stolen motorboat and sat down behind the wheel.

"All set?" the chief officer asked him.

"Yes, sir."

The commander of the launch now turned to Ned and ordered, "You all come along with us, too!"

· 13 ·

Bats !

GEORGE and Burt continued to argue with the river police but to no avail. Finally George said, "The boat our friends are in is being rented by the hour. Please, can't we return it before going to headquarters?"

The chief officer consented.

"Thank you," said George. She hoped that by contacting the man from whom they had rented the boat, the group of young people would be exonerated.

Her hopes were in vain. Although the man did identify them as the group who had rented one of his boats, he said he had no idea where they were going. For all he knew they might have rented his boat to steal the other one. Ned paid him for the use of the *Water Witch*, then he Nancy, Bess, and Dave climbed aboard the officers' launch.

It proceeded to the police jetty. Here the six friends were ushered into a building which was a branch of the main police headquarters. All of them were questioned. Finally Nancy said, "I'm the Nancy Drew whose car was stolen."

"Yes, we know," the officer in charge said. "It hasn't been found yet."

"Now that you know who we are, and that we're not boat thieves, may we please go?"

"Not yet. You haven't proved that you didn't take the boat we found two of you in."

"We have no proof," Nancy replied. "But also you have no proof we stole the boat."

The officer looked searchingly at her. "You sound like a lawyer."

"Probably I've learned that from my father. He's Carson Drew of River Heights—a lawyer."

Suddenly the officer's face broke into a wide grin. "Carson Drew? Everybody knows him. So you're his daughter? Why didn't you tell the river police that in the first place?"

Nancy did not answer. She merely smiled, and the officer said with a wink, "Case dismissed."

When the young people reached the sidewalk outside, Dave came alongside Nancy and rubbed his arm against hers. "Boy, am I glad to be a friend of such a famous person!"

Everyone laughed and the gay mood of the group was restored. When they sobered again, George said, "That fellow who tried to ram us must have stolen the boat just for that reason."

"I wonder who he is," Bess mused.

The following morning Nancy and her friends went to church, then drove in Ned's car to the castle. As they went down the tree-shaded lane, Nancy and George were delighted to discover that the drawbridge was still down. Even the stones they had heaped on it were in place.

"Just the same, I'm going to leave my car on this side," said Ned.

Burt chuckled. "Now we won't have to use those swimming trunks we brought."

"And I was planning on being a gallant knight and letting the drawbridge down for miladies to cross!" said Dave.

Nancy and George grinned and showed how they had anchored the bridge so that it could not be raised from inside the castle.

"Clever," said Ned.

The visitors hurried across and walked into the cobblestoned courtyard which was filled with tufts of grass and weeds that even grew through cracks in the porticoes. Nancy and Ned decided to start their search at the tower end of the castle. They found that on the ground floor, directly below the tower, was a mammoth baronial hall. There was nothing in it but a collection of many years of dust and cobwebs.

"This must have been gorgeous," said George, as she and Burt joined the others in the great room.

In order not to miss finding anyone who might be hiding out in the castle, the young people separated into three pairs, each taking a section. They walked through room after room, some of which opened off adjoining suites and others only off the porticoes. Finally the six friends met back in the great hall.

"Did you find anything?" each excitedly asked the other. But none of them had.

George added, "No bed, cooker, food, or clothing to indicate anyone is living here."

The searchers had noticed three stairways leading to

the floor above—a wide one from the baronial hall, and two narrow ones in other sections. Each couple took one of them to the first floor. Here they found a series of rooms, some with doors, many of them missing.

"I presume lots of things have been stolen from here by souvenir hunters and vandals," Nancy surmised.

"I'm afraid so," said Ned. "It's a shame this beautiful place is being allowed to go to ruin."

When the other two couples joined them, George reported that she and Burt had come upon a locked door. They did not know whether it opened into a room or possibly to a stairway leading to the tower.

Nancy was excited. "Maybe someone is living in the tower!" she suggested. "Our bearded friend!"

George led the way to the heavy oak door. There was a wooden slide bolt on it, but this was open. Still the door would not give.

Ned and Burt took hold of the enormous knob on it and gave a tremendous heave. This time the door opened, but the young people fell back in dismay from a dark stairway ahead of them.

They were about to be attacked by a flock of bats!

The group took to their heels. Nancy, at the end of the line, kept pace with Ned. Presently she looked around to see what had become of the bats. To her amazement, she saw a man come from the tower stairway and run down the hall in the opposite direction.

"Ned!" she cried, grabbing his arm and stopping short. "I saw that tower signaller! Let's chase him!"

She called to the rest of her friends to turn back and follow them, but they did not hear her. She and Ned started running down the hall after the man.

As they turned a corner, Nancy saw him reach one of the smaller stairways and start downwards.

"Stop!" she cried out. "We're not going to harm you! We just want to talk to you!"

The stranger paid no attention and disappeared. Nancy and Ned raced after him, but by the time they reached the ground floor he was out of sight.

"We'd better separate if we hope to find him," said Nancy.

"All right, but be careful," Ned agreed.

The two hurried off in opposite directions. In a few moments Nancy came to an open doorway. Before her was a circular, enclosed stairway leading to the cellar. The steps were of stone, but the walls were oak panelled.

"That man must have gone down to the cellar," Nancy decided. "This door wasn't open the first time we examined this floor." She glanced at the door. It matched the panelling of the hallway exactly and at first glance might not have been noticed. Apparently the searchers had missed it.

As Nancy listened, she was sure she heard a creaking noise below her. Was the man just reaching the cellar, or was he hiding some place and causing a door to creak?

At that moment Ned joined her and she pointed below. In a whisper she said, "I think he's down there. Let's go!"

Ned laid a restraining hand on her arm. "Not you. I'll go."

It was only then that Nancy realized how dark it was below. "You couldn't find your way," she said.

Ned grinned. From his trouser pocket he pulled a

flashlight. "You've taught me this much about sleuthing. Never go on a search in dark places without a light. I'll go first. If everything's okay, you follow," he said.

Ned went slowly down the winding stairway. Presently he was out of sight. Nancy waited anxiously, hoping there would be no attack by the bearded man or other persons.

"Okay," he called up a moment later. "Come ahead!"

As Nancy started down, Ned began a search for the man. Suddenly he realized that Nancy was taking a very long time to descend the stairway.

"Nancy!" he called. "What's wrong?"

There was no answer. Worried, Ned hurried up the stairway. Not only was Nancy not on it, but when he reached the ground floor he discovered that she was not in sight.

Bess and George and the boys hurried towards him. "Where's Nancy?" they asked in one breath.

"I don't know," Ned said fearfully, then told them where he had left her.

"When was that?" Bess asked quickly.

"Why, just a few minutes ago."

"Then she didn't come up the stairway, nor was she anywhere near it," said Bess. "Otherwise, we would have seen her."

The five young people looked at one another. Panic seized them. What had happened to Nancy?

· 14 ·

The Castle Captive

"I SHOULDN'T have left Nancy alone!" Ned declared, blaming himself for her disappearance.

"Let's talk about this sensibly," said George.

The group discussed the situation for several minutes and concluded that Nancy could not have left the castle.

"Since she didn't go upstairs," said George, "that leaves only one place she could be—the cellar."

"But why didn't I see her?" Ned argued. "I suggest you girls wait here. Burt and Dave and I will go downstairs with a flashlight and see what we can find out."

Ned tried to keep his voice calm but the others knew he was greatly upset. He led the way and presently the boys vanished into the darkness of the castle basement.

Bess and George stood at the top of the stairway looking up and down the long corridor and hoping Nancy would reappear. George strode back and forth nervously. Bess was dabbing her tear-filled eyes with a handkerchief.

Finally George said, "I can't stand this any longer. The boys should have been back by this time. Maybe something has happened to them too!"

She started down the cellar stairway. Bess went after her and grabbed her arm. "If we all get captured, who's going to go for help?" she asked.

"You're right," George agreed. "But what in the world happened to Nancy? It seems as if she just vanished into thin air."

Bess gave a tremendous sigh. "That moonstone somebody sent her certainly didn't help Nancy. I'd say it brought her *bad* luck."

As Bess stopped speaking, both girls heard a startled mutter. It seemed to be coming out of the wall!

The cousins huddled together. Who had made the sound? The two girls gazed at the panelled beams beside them. Was it possible someone was hidden behind the wooden wall?

George decided someone was there. Could the person be Nancy—trapped, injured, or a prisoner? Was someone with her, keeping the young sleuth from crying out? The girls must find the answer!

Motioning with her hands, George indicated a plan to Bess, who nodded. George would go down to the cellar, try to find the boys, and get them to help break down the wall. Although Bess was fearful of being left alone, she consented. Her heart was pounding like a hammer.

On tiptoe George went down the rest of the flight. When her eyes became accustomed to the dimness, she started walking ahead. To her relief, she saw the three boys coming back. They had not been harmed!

Burt said in a scolding tone, "It's dangerous down here! Why didn't you stay upstairs?"

George paid no attention to the question, but quickly whispered what she and Bess had heard. "I suggest we tiptoe back up and you boys examine the wall where the muttering came from. There's something creepy going on there."

Cautiously the four ascended the steps. Ned beamed his flashlight over the panelled wall. Suddenly he pointed to the well-concealed latch of a two-panelled door.

He motioned for Bess and George to go to the top of the stairway. As he held the flashlight on the door, Burt and Dave silently moved the latch and yanked the door open.

Out tumbled Nancy!

She fell limply into Ned's arms. For a few seconds all eyes were on Nancy, then Burt looked again at the door from which Nancy had emerged. A large cupboard was revealed. In it stood a bearded man, stunned by the sudden turn of events, and unable to escape from his captors.

"Just *who* are you?" Burt cried, grabbing the man's arm.

As he yanked him from the cupboard, both of them lost their balance and went rolling down the stairway. Dave went flying after the tumbling figures. Bess and George could hear a scuffle going on below.

Meanwhile, Ned had picked Nancy up and now carried her outdoors. The fresh air quickly revived her.

"Oh, Nancy," said Bess, coming outside, "what happened?"

Between long breaths of air, Nancy explained that as she was descending the cellar stairway, suddenly the secret door had burst open, startling her. The man had grabbed her and held a vial under her nose. The fumes from the vial had made her dizzy and she was unable to escape. "Then he yanked me into the cupboard and closed the door."

"Oh, you poor thing!" said Bess.

Presently Burt and Dave arrived with their captive. He glowered at the young people. "Now tell your story," Ned ordered him.

The prisoner only glared. They asked him his name, but he refused to give it. He would not say whether or not he was living at the castle.

Ned put his hand into the man's pocket and brought out a vial. He read the label and gave a sigh of relief. "This stuff is perfectly harmless," he said. "It'll just make a person sleepy." Turning to the prisoner, he asked, "Are you in the habit of carrying this with you?"

"A guy's got a right to some protection," the man grumbled, then he ignored further questions put to him as to why he was living there.

Nancy, who now felt quite like herself, said, "I'm rather glad this man abducted me. Otherwise, we wouldn't have any excuse for taking him to the police."

"Police!" the man shrieked. "You ain't goin' to take me to the police! I ain't done nothin'! This girl was too snoopy. I had to keep her quiet."

This time he was ignored by the young people. Burt and Dave offered to drive the prisoner to town and turn him over to the authorities, then come back for the others.

"Fine," said Nancy. "I'd like to investigate that tower."

"No! No! You mustn't do that!" the prisoner cried out. "You can't go up there!"

"Why not?" Nancy asked.

"It's dangerous! You'll get into trouble!" the man replied.

"Come on!" Burt urged the man. He and Dave took their captive by his arms and hurried him towards Ned's car.

"Oh, here are the car keys," said Ned, running forward to hand them to Dave.

When he returned, Ned asked Nancy if she really felt well enough to make the ascent to the turret. She insisted that she did, so Ned and the three girls returned to the castle and climbed to the third floor.

"I hope we don't meet those bats again," said Bess fearfully. "If this turret is their home, they may come back before we leave."

"We will have to take that chance," George told her.

Bess said no more. The door to the tower was still open and the young people climbed the stairs. Above was a stone-walled circular room. It contained a bed, a small paraffin stove, a table, and a chair.

"That old man has been living here all right," Ned remarked.

Nancy had been casting her eyes around, looking for an opening to the roof of the turret. On one wall, in a corner, was an iron ladder. Above it, she could discern a trap door. Nancy pointed it out to the others, and Ned started up the ladder.

"Nothing out here but a space to stand on," he called down.

"Any clues?" Nancy asked.

Ned looked around and reported that he could find nothing. As he descended, Nancy began a search of the room. Under the bed she saw a piece of paper and reached down to pick it up. On it were typed the words:

Our password will be Moonstone Valley.

When the others saw it, Bess gave a start. "Moonstone Valley again!" she exclaimed. "Nancy, that man wasn't fooling when he told you it was dangerous to come up here. This must be the hideout of some gang."

"You're right," George added. "And they know the old name for this area."

Nancy was thoughtful. Now she was sure that the castle, the bearded man, the moonstone she had received, and some nefarious gang were all connected somehow. But who were the gang members? Mr Seaman and friends of his?

She and the others searched the room thoroughly but could find no other clue. In the distance they heard a car and assumed the boys were returning.

"Let's go!" Bess said nervously.

The group trudged back to the drawbridge, where Burt and Dave met them. The boys reported that the prisoner was behind bars.

"The chief wants to talk to you, Nancy, after lunch," said Burt.

At the mention of the word "lunch", the young people realized how hungry they were. George, who at

once suggested the Brass Kettle, told Burt and Dave
that she would introduce them to a gossipy but nice old
lady. At first the girls' escorts frowned, but when they
heard that Mrs Hemstead had really helped in ad-
vancing the solution of the mystery, the boys relented.

To the girls' amazement, the elderly woman was not
in her usual place. The rocking chair was empty and
Mrs Hemstead's daughter said that her mother was not
feeling well and had remained in her room.

Nancy expressed her sympathy and led the way into
the tearoom. As soon as lunch was over, the six friends
walked to the police station. Chief Burke asked Nancy
to prefer charges against her assailant.

"He still won't give his name and he has no money
on him," the official said.

Nancy consented, and signed the prescribed form.

"Oh, dear!" said Bess. "I wish it hadn't been neces-
sary for you to do that. I'm sure now the Moonstone
Valley gang will be after you!"

Chief Burke's eyebrows lifted. "Moonstone Valley
gang?" he repeated. "That's one gang I haven't
heard of. What do you know about them?"

Nancy produced the typed slip which she had found
in the prisoner's bedroom. The officer was amazed and
requested that she leave the paper with him. "This calls
for a police investigation," he declared. "But I'm glad
you sightseers learned about this fellow."

"When you searched the prisoner," the young sleuth
said, "did you find anything of special interest on
him?"

Chief Burke opened a drawer in his desk and pulled
out a dirty piece of white paper. "Only this," he said.

"It might be a clue to something, but it doesn't make sense to me."

"What does it say?" Nancy inquired.

The officer handed the paper to her. The instant Nancy saw the two words, she was sure this was a code signal. It read:

Wolf's Eye.

· 15 ·

An Exciting Photograph

NEITHER Nancy nor the police detectives could shed any light on the mysterious words "Wolf's Eye".

"But please let me know if you find out what it means," Nancy requested. "Also, if your prisoner talks —or if you have any word about my stolen car."

Chief Burke promised, adding that he was sorry that his men had not been able to pick up one single lead on Nancy's convertible.

"I certainly do miss it," said Nancy. "But right now we have transportation." She looked gratefully at Ned and the officer smiled.

When Nancy and her friends reached the motel, Mrs Thompson said that Jody Armstrong had been trying all day to get in touch with them.

"She wants you girls to come to a picnic at her home."

"That's sweet of her," said Nancy. "I'll call her right away."

Out of earshot of the others, Nancy telephoned Jody. After thanking her for the invitation, Nancy said that three friends of hers were there for the night, so she would not be able to accept.

"Oh, bring them along!" said Jody. "The more the merrier!"

"Is this a picnic party just for girls?" Nancy asked hesitantly.

"Oh, no," Jody replied. "It's a mixed party!" She giggled. "Are your friends boys?"

"Yes, they are."

"Wonderful!" Jody cried joyfully. "I'll expect you all at seven."

The boys were delighted. Ned remarked with a twinkle in his eye, "I'll be glad to see you relax for once, Nancy. I'm sure there won't be any mystery at the picnic."

The three girls looked at one another. They said nothing to the boys, but were hopeful that they would pick up a clue there regarding Jody Armstrong's adoption.

The Armstrong back garden was large and very attractive. There was a beautiful velvet-green lawn surrounded by deep flower beds. The scent of roses pervaded the warm night air.

At one side was a long buffet table with tempting salad bowls and snacks. There was a large punch bowl in the centre brimming with ice-cold punch. Farther along at the side of the garden was a stone fireplace for outdoor cooking. A boy about eighteen years old stood there, grinning. He wore a large white apron and a chef's cap.

Many young people had already gathered when Nancy and her friends arrived. Jody, a gracious hostess, immediately introduced the group. When they came to the chef, Jody giggled. "This is my cousin, Harvey

Smith. He's the best cook-out chef in the county. Isn't he a riot in that outfit?"

Harvey acknowledged the introduction and said, chuckling, "It's one way to get yourself invited to all the parties!"

Nancy, Ned, and the others seated themselves on mats on the ground with the other guests. They thoroughly enjoyed the evening. Burt declared that Harvey's steaks were the best he had ever eaten. The rest of the menu included crisps, several kinds of salad, vanilla ice cream topped with fresh fruit, and cake.

"I'm stuffed!" Dave said with a groan, as he finished the last crumb of cake.

As he spoke, the strumming of a guitar could be heard. Looking up, the River Heights visitors and their escorts saw a young man standing at the edge of the crowd. The musician began to sing. First came a humorous song about a hillbilly and his first shop-bought shoes. Each verse ended with "Ow! They pinch! Ow! They hurt!"

Soon he was playing familiar songs. Everyone at the picnic joined in. This was followed by a sidesplitting skit put on by one of the couples. They represented two travellers who had met on a cruise. They could not speak each other's language, but each was trying to tell the other how to get back to the same hotel!

Before anyone realized the time, one of Jody's friends said, "My goodness! It's almost twelve o'clock!"

That seemed to be a signal for everyone to leave. Nancy and her friends went to say goodnight to their hostess.

When Nancy reached Jody, the girl said, "Oh, please

don't go yet. I have something upstairs I want to show you. Wait until all the other guests except your friends have gone. My cousin wants to talk to them, anyway."

"All right."

Nancy and her friends walked over towards a particularly beautiful part of the flower garden. There were a couple of benches here, and they all sat down. Harvey Smith joined them.

Presently the last of the other guests had said good night. Jody came over and beckoned to Nancy. To the others she said, "I won't keep her long."

The two girls went upstairs to Jody's bedroom, which was dainty and girlish with its white muslin curtains and hand-embroidered bedspread.

"Mother said that when you were here yesterday you mentioned childhood pictures of me," Jody began. "Well, we hadn't looked at them in ages, so just for a laugh, I went up to the attic last night and unearthed them. Would you still like to see them?"

"Oh, yes," Nancy responded.

Most of the pictures were in boxes. The first one Jody picked up held photographs of her at the age of twelve. There was nothing about this girl that looked like the three-year-old whose photograph Nancy had in her bag.

"I guess you were always cute," said Nancy, smiling. She mentioned the dress Jody was wearing in the picture and the two girls laughed over it.

"You wouldn't think styles for kids would change so quickly," Jody remarked. "And my hair! A twelve-year-old today wouldn't look a bit like that!"

Jody kept going backwards in time, as Nancy con-

cealed her impatience. But finally she reached the last
box and said, "These pictures were taken soon after my
mother and father adopted me." Jody smiled. "Adopted
children are very lucky because they're chosen and
keenly wanted by their adoptive parents."

Nancy agreed and added that the Armstrongs were
wonderful people. "You're fortunate to have found one
another."

At that moment Mrs Armstrong called Jody. "Will
you please come downstairs for a minute, dear?" she
asked.

"Of course, Mother." Jody turned to Nancy. "I
won't be away long. You go right ahead looking at the
pictures."

Nancy was delighted to be left alone. Quickly she
opened the last box and picked up a photograph. Her
pulse quickened as she opened her bag and took out the
picture of Joanie Horton taken only about six months
before the other one.

This was the same child!

"Jody Armstrong and Joanie Horton *are* the same
person!" Nancy thought. "Her mother didn't leave her
under mysterious circumstances! Her parents weren't
living. She *was* kidnapped! I'm sure Jody and Mr and
Mrs Armstrong will want to know the truth. And it will
bring such happiness to the Bowens to know that their
granddaughter is alive and happy!

"And Jody is the rightful heir to Mrs Horton's estate!
That twenty-one-year-old girl who claimed it brought
forged identification papers with her from New
York!"

Many suppositions raced through Nancy's mind

First of all, she must keep her findings a secret until she could talk to her father. Who was behind the whole scheme? Who had kidnapped little Joanie and left her at the adoption society? The girl who later impersonated her or someone else? Where was that girl now? In San Francisco? Was any of the estate money left after all this time?

"One thing is sure," Nancy told herself. "The people responsible for this deception are determined I'm not going to upset anything." She chuckled. "But I've uncovered their evil scheme."

Suddenly she heard Jody coming back upstairs. Quickly Nancy tucked her own photograph of Joanie Horton into her bag.

As Jody walked into the room, Nancy said, "Thanks a million for showing me the pictures. You were a darling to go to all that trouble. And now, I guess I'd better not keep my friends waiting any longer."

Nancy kept the secret to herself until the young people had driven back to the motel and the girls had said good night to the boys. Then, when she was in her room with Bess and George, Nancy told them the exciting news.

"Oh, Nancy, you are absolutely marvellous!" Bess said. "Now Jody can learn the truth and get all that money."

George took a more practical view of the matter. "There may not be one cent of it left," she said. "I think it would be better if matters stay the way they are and Jody never finds out."

"No matter what we do," said Nancy, "you *must* help me keep this a secret."

Her friends promised, then Bess asked, "What are you going to do?"

Nancy said that at this point she thought her father should take over the case. "He'll decide what is the best move to make. Dad will know how to break the news to the Bowens and see what they want to do."

"Now that you've solved the case, I suppose we'll go home," Bess remarked.

"Oh, no," Nancy said quickly. "I haven't solved anything except the identification of Jody Armstrong. Don't forget that her grandmother's estate was stolen. Now we have to concentrate on unravelling that mystery."

Bess and George knew that Nancy suspected Mr Seaman, the other mysterious man who had followed her, and the bearded fellow they had caught in the castle. Both girls said they would stay with her and continue their work.

The three friends were up early to say goodbye to the boys. Ned and the other boys begged the girls to be careful in their sleuthing.

"I'm mighty glad we were here to help you capture that fellow," said Ned. "But don't try going to that castle by yourselves!"

Nancy smiled. "Next time I'll take a handsome young policeman," she teased.

As soon as the boys had driven off, Nancy went to the phone and tried to reach her father. But he still had not returned to the San Francisco hotel. She then phoned her home in River Heights. She told Hannah Gruen of her exciting discovery and asked the housekeeper to try reaching Mr Drew in California to give him the information.

"I'll keep trying," the housekeeper promised. "It's too bad I didn't know this yesterday. Your father phoned last night—said he had tried you at the Long View, but learned you were out and didn't leave his name. So he gave me some interesting information to pass along to you."

"What is it?" Nancy asked quickly.

Mrs Gruen said that Mr Drew had tracked down a Joanie Horton who had come from the East. "She is now married to a John Taber. Your father didn't have any further details, but I think he's going to try to see this woman."

"She may be the impostor!" Nancy said excitedly.

"It looks that way," Hannah Gruen agreed. "My goodness, Nancy, this case may be drawing to a close!"

"Oh, wouldn't it be wonderful?" Nancy exclaimed.

"In any event, I'll be glad when you come back home," the housekeeper said wistfully. "It's too quiet here."

"I'm sure it won't be long," Nancy said cheerfully. "Well, 'bye for now."

When Nancy relayed the information to Bess and George, they too were excited. "Well, what course shall we follow, Captain Drew?" George asked.

Nancy thought for a moment, then answered, "Let's have an early lunch at the Brass Kettle. If Mrs Hemstead is there, I'll ask her if Mr Seaman has been around."

"But we haven't even had breakfast yet," Bess spoke

up. "What are we going to do between now and lunchtime?"

Nancy suggested that a walk would do the girls good. "Let's hike down to that restaurant."

The girls ate a tasty breakfast, then Nancy said, "How about going over to police headquarters to see if Chief Burke has any news?"

The three girls hurried to headquarters. They were shown at once to the police chief's office.

Chief Burke looked up and said genially, "You must be mind readers. I was just going to get in touch with you."

"Do you have news for us?" Nancy asked.

"Yes, indeed. Your prisoner has talked!"

· 16 ·

Reptile Guard

"THE prisoner has confessed?" Nancy eagerly asked the police chief.

"Not completely," the officer replied. "But he did tell us his name. It's Jake Suggs."

"And he was living at the castle?"

"Yes."

Chief Burke went on to say that the prisoner had suddenly called one of the guards and cried out, "I'm not goin' to be responsible for a murder!"

Nancy's eyes widened in wonder as did those of Bess and George. "Murder!" Nancy repeated.

"That's what he said," Chief Burke continued. "Then this man Suggs said, 'There's a man hidden in the cellar of the castle. He's sick! If you don't get him out of there, he'll die!' "

"Did you get him out?" Bess asked breathlessly.

The officer nodded. "And now here's the big surprise. The prisoner in the cellar was Mr Wheeler!"

The girls were dumbfounded. Finally Nancy found her voice to say, "Thank goodness! How is he?"

Chief Burke said that Mr Wheeler had been taken to the hospital and was now under heavy guard. He had been fed and well cared for by Suggs, but was too weak to escape.

"Did you learn anything else from either Mr Wheeler or Suggs?" Nancy queried.

"Not a thing. Mr Wheeler evidently was put to sleep before he was taken from the hospital and knew nothing more until he awakened in a dark room in the castle cellar. No one had questioned him, and except for the care Suggs gave him, the retired lawyer was left alone. Suggs merely said some people brought Mr Wheeler to the castle and paid him to take care of the lawyer."

"Who were they?" Nancy asked.

"I wish I knew," said Chief Burke.

Then the officer's stern expression relaxed and he smiled slightly. "I thought you might be interested in Suggs's story about the bats," he said. "He let them remain there to frighten away any intruders."

Bess giggled. "They did that all right," she said, hunching her shoulders reminiscently in disgust.

The chief turned to Nancy. "Miss Detective, have you any idea who brought Mr Wheeler to the castle?"

"I'm afraid not. But I'd certainly like to find them."

"I'll bet Nancy *will* find them!" George spoke up.

Nancy now said that she thought Suggs knew much more than he was telling. "For instance, before Mr Wheeler was kidnapped, George and I went to the castle and were warned away when we were about to enter. Furthermore, we saw a car leaving there that same day. Also, through binoculars I used on the hill, I saw Suggs signalling from the tower. The day Suggs was captured my friend Ned Nickerson was searching in the cellar and didn't see Mr Wheeler."

"That's not surprising," said the officer. "Mr Wheeler was in a room with a well-camouflaged door."

He went on to say that the police were still searching for the kidnappers, of course, but had to admit they did not have a single lead and Suggs refused to give names. "And I'm afraid we have no word on your car, Miss Drew."

Nancy had a sudden idea. She knew the chief would think it far fetched, since he had no notion she connected the mystery of Mr Wheeler's abduction with the mystery about which he knew nothing—that of Joanie Horton's kidnapping. Aloud she said, "If there's a gang around here hiding things at the castle, maybe my convertible is there."

Even Bess and George were surprised to hear this. George reminded Nancy that not only had the girls and boys searched the castle, but also that the police had.

"But they didn't search the grounds," Nancy countered.

"That's true," Chief Burke admitted.

Nancy asked him if he could spare any officers to go out to the castle with the girls and look around. He agreed and said he would send Sergeant Fosley and Detective Humfrey with them. The men were called in and introduced, then they led the girls outside to a police car.

The group set off for the castle. When they reached it, Nancy was glad to find the drawbridge still down. She had half expected that when Suggs's friends failed to see him signalling, they would have come to find out why. The first thing they would do would be to remove the stones and wires holding down the drawbridge and hope to avoid a further search of their secret meeting place by the police. What had happened? Were they afraid to return?

The driver parked on the narrow roadway beside the wall, then the three girls and two police officers began a thorough and systematic search of the grounds. They had concluded there were plenty of places in which a person might hide a car. Tall grass and weeds grew everywhere. The searchers combed the sides and back of the castle.

Presently George called, "I see flattened grass—two narrow rows of it. They could be from car tyres."

Nancy and Bess ran to her side. There was no mistaking the tracks, although the weeds and grass were struggling to an upright position again.

Excited, the girls followed the trail. Presently they reached a slightly depressed area at the end of which was a huge mound of grass. Embedded into the hill was an enormous wooden door.

"Your car could be in there!" Bess called over her shoulder to Nancy.

Bess was in the lead. But suddenly she stopped and shrieked, "Ugh! A snake—a monstrous snake!"

Nancy and George looked at the ground. In front of the door, sunning itself on some rocks, was a five-foot snake. At the sound of the girls' approach, the reptile raised its head. The forked tongue shot out from its mouth.

"Car or no car, I'm not staying!" said Bess, who started to retreat.

George, unafraid, looked round for a rock to throw near the snake and scare it away. "He's just guarding the place," she said with a chuckle.

"I can't see what's so funny about that," her cousin retorted, but she stopped running.

By this time George had found a small rock and heaved it towards the reptile. It landed within a few inches of the smooth body. At once the snake slithered off through the grass.

The police, having heard the shouts, and Bess's scream, had come from the other side of the castle at a run. By the time they caught up to the girls, Nancy was pulling at the old door. It proved to be too heavy for her to move.

At once Sergeant Fosley and Detective Humfrey stepped forward and gave it a yank. As the huge door opened, Nancy gave a cry of glee. "My car!" she cried.

The young sleuth ran inside the large opening and climbed behind the wheel of her convertible. There was no key in the ignition lock but she had hers in her bag. Quickly she inserted it into the lock and a second later had started the engine.

"It runs!" she exclaimed, smiling broadly.

The two officers looked on in amazement. Then Sergeant Fosley said, "You are a clever young sleuth! No one else thought of looking on this island for your car!"

There was a short discussion about the thieves who had taken it. Everyone doubted that they planned to use it or sell it. They reached the conclusion that the car had been taken to keep Nancy from sleuthing in the neighbourhood!

"Apparently you have a reputation all the way up here in Deep River," said Detective Humfrey. "Well, now that you have your car, I guess you don't need us any longer. We'd better get back, Fosley."

The two men hurried off to their own car. They waited, however, to see that Nancy's convertible was still running all right. Then they crossed the drawbridge and sped off.

"Let's look around here some more," Nancy suggested. "With luck, maybe we'll find some clues to the identity of Suggs's pals!"

"Not on your life," Bess retorted. "Nancy Drew, don't forget your promise to Ned."

Nancy gave a sigh of resignation. She had just driven on to the drawbridge when the girls heard creaking, groaning sounds in the wood beneath them. The next second the bridge began to lift!

Bess screamed. "Nancy! The bridge is opening! We'll be thrown off!"

· 17 ·

Tell-tale Tracks

As THE drawbridge rose creakingly, Nancy put her car engine into reverse, sped backwards down the incline, and into the courtyard. She was just in time to keep the convertible from turning over or being crushed.

"Nancy, don't give me a scare like that again!" Bess begged.

Her cousin looked at her disdainfully. "You'd think it was Nancy's fault. We're lucky to be alive, thanks to her."

Bess apologized, saying she had not meant to imply that Nancy was a poor driver. To forestall an argument, Nancy said, "What on earth made the bridge rise?"

The three girls climbed out of the car. They looked at the bridge, which was not tightly in place in the castle wall.

"The bridge certainly wouldn't go up by itself," said George, "unless the vibration of the policemen's car loosened the wires and released the secret mechanism."

"This means we're prisoners here, unless we leave the the car and swim across," said Bess with a sigh.

"Not necessarily," Nancy told her. "Maybe I can let the drawbridge down."

"How about the police?" Bess asked suddenly. "Maybe if we honk the horn loudly enough, they'll come back."

She moved towards the car to do this. But though Bess kept her hand on the horn for half a minute, there was no response.

George and Nancy had moved to the drawbridge. Together, they tugged and yanked at the heavy iron chains which let the bridge up and down. One side worked, but the other refused to budge.

"I think the trouble's up above where the chain goes through the wall," Nancy stated. "I'll go and find out."

"But how?" George asked. "You can't climb up a sheer wall."

Nancy smiled. "But look at the steplike niches in the stonework," she said. "They might be just the trick."

"Okay," said George, "but what are you going to hold on to?"

"There are some pretty heavy creepers on this wall," Nancy observed. The next moment she had grasped a stout stem of the ivy. She swung herself on to it to try its strength. "It'll hold me all right," she said.

Quickly Nancy inched her way up the wall, using the vines and niches. When she reached the top of the drawbridge, she began to examine the bulky chain and the cogwheel over which it ran. Nancy discovered that the chain was wound around two of the teeth in such a way that the wheel could not turn and release the bridge.

Holding on to the vine stem firmly with one hand, the young sleuth endeavoured to lift the chain and unwind it. At first she could not budge the heavy iron links, and once she almost lost her balance.

"Be careful!" George warned. "Want me to come up and help?"

"Maybe you'd better," said Nancy. "But whatever you do, pick out a different vine from mine!"

George chuckled and followed instructions. "I knew being a tomboy would come in handy some day!" she called, as she made her ascent. Soon she was beside her chum.

The two girls worked hard. But they did not dare tug too strenuously for fear that the force would unbalance them in their precarious positions. Finally they managed to get the links back into the cogs in a straight line.

"Thank goodness!" said George.

Nancy heaved a sigh. "I'm pretty relieved myself. Now all we have to do is see if it works."

George grinned. "And I suppose you'd like *me* to climb down and test it." She descended and released the two chains. At once the drawbridge was lowered.

"That's simply marvellous!" cried Bess. "You girls are positive geniuses."

"Anyway," said George, "we're not such bad mechanics."

When Nancy reached the ground, she insisted that the cousins walk across the bridge. "I'll come alone in the car. If anything goes wrong again, you can hurry off for help."

Bess and George waited with bated breath, but Nancy made it safely. Her friends climbed into the convertible and she drove towards town.

"I'm starved," said Bess. "Adventure always makes me hungry."

George laughed. "Tension is supposed to take away your appetite," she said, "not increase it!"

Nancy suggested that they head for the Brass Kettle. "Maybe Mrs Hemstead will give us some more information about Mr Seaman."

When they entered the tearoom, the girls were delighted to see the old lady rocking in her chair. At once she motioned to them.

"I haven't had a soul to talk to all morning," she complained. "Tell me what you've been doing."

"We've been out for a drive," Nancy said nonchalantly. "You know, Mrs Hemstead, I never have received the present from Mr Seaman that he told you about. Has he been here lately?"

"No, he hasn't," Mrs Hemstead replied. "But you know, I heard a funny thing about him."

Instantly the girls were alert and asked her what it was.

The old lady rocked determinedly as if she were angry. "He fooled me—that's what he did," she said. "All this time I thought he was a travelling salesman, but I was told just last night that he's working out at old Mrs Wilson's."

The girls could hardly suppress smiles. Mrs Hemstead felt that she had been duped, and did not like it! She went on to say that Mrs Wilson was a wealthy widow who lived on the outskirts of Deep River.

"Up to a short time ago," Mrs Hemstead continued, "Mrs Wilson kept four servants, but now she has only a couple. I suppose the woman is Mr Seaman's wife. Mrs Wilson never comes to town any more. There are rumours around here she's not well."

"That's too bad," Nancy said sympathetically. "Do Mr and Mrs Seaman take care of her?"

"I suppose so," Mrs Hemstead said. "Folks don't know what's going on out there any more. The couple never come to town, either. They order all their food and supplies by telephone. Funny thing, too, the delivery boys never see anybody. The money is left outside in the milk box."

Instantly Nancy's mind flew back to the similar story about Grandmother Horton. Could the Seamans be the same couple she had had? Nancy told herself she was going to follow up this clue at once As casually as possible she asked Mrs Hemstead the location of Mrs Wilson's home.

"Well, when you get out on the main road, you take the road towards the old castle. After you pass the castle, take the next road to the left that you come to. Mrs Wilson's house is way down at the end near the water."

The three girls explained that they wanted to have lunch and said goodbye to Mrs Hemstead. As soon as they were seated and had ordered their luncheon, Nancy told Bess and George that she wanted to go out to the Wilson home directly after the girls finished eating.

About an hour later Nancy drove within sight of the Wilson house. She decided to hide her car along the wooded roadside.

"Let's walk up the Wilson driveway and try not to make ourselves conspicuous," she cautioned. Fortunately, the drive was a curving one, bordered by trees and thick shrubbery.

Suddenly George exclaimed, "Look! Tyre tracks

that don't match. They're just like the ones we saw at
the castle!"

The girls stooped to examine them. Three of the
tyres had parallel grooves; the one on the right rear
wheel was diamond-shaped.

"We're on the trail of something all right," Bess
remarked. "But let's not get ourselves captured!"

They hurried along the side of the road, ready to hide
among the trees and bushes if a car should come along
or any people appear. They neared the end of the driveway, where the trees on the far side ended, and a long
green lawn extended for some distance.

"Girls!" Nancy whispered tensely. She pointed to
their left. The tower of Moonstone Castle was in plain
view! "Anyone standing here could have watched
Jake Suggs signalling!"

"O-oh!" said Bess. "I've seen enough! Let's go back!"

"No!" said Nancy. "We have a real clue this time."
She came from behind a tree, walked up to the front
door, and boldly lifted the big brass knocker.

· 18 ·

Worried Plotters

WHEN there was no answer to Nancy's knock, she tried
again. Still no one came to open the door of Mrs
Wilson's home.

Disappointed, Nancy was about to turn away, when
Bess rushed up to her. She had been standing some distance back from the house and had been gazing at the
windows. Now she exclaimed in an excited whisper:

"Somebody *is* home. I saw a middle-aged woman
looking out one of the upstairs windows."

"Middle-aged?" George repeated. "That couldn't
be old Mrs Wilson."

"That's right," Nancy agreed. "I wonder why the
woman doesn't come and answer my knock?"

"Maybe she's deaf," George suggested, and ran back
from the doorway so that she would be in plain view if
anyone looked out of the window again.

Nancy, meanwhile, hammered the door knocker
vigorously. No one came to answer it.

"Evidently they don't want to see us," said Bess.

The three girls discussed the question of whether it
was just they who were not welcome, or whether no
callers were allowed into the house. They did not come
to any conclusion.

"Why don't we pretend to leave?" said Nancy. "We'll go down the driveway a short distance and double back, using the trees as a screen."

She and the cousins followed this plan and remained in hiding for nearly ten minutes. They had a good view of the house, but no one appeared at any of the windows, or came to open the door.

"We may as well go," said Bess.

"Not yet," Nancy begged. "I see a way to get up to the house without being spotted. Normally I dislike eavesdropping, but in this case I think it is justified."

The young sleuth managed to make her way behind trees and among bushes to an open, screened window not far from the front door. She had barely settled into a comfortable listening position when a car came up the driveway.

At once Bess was terrified. "Now we'll be caught!" she told George.

"Sh!" her cousin warned and pulled Bess down to a stooping position. "Nancy's well out of sight. I'm sure nobody will see her."

As the car went past the place where the cousins were hiding, they could see the lone driver plainly. He was the man who had followed Nancy in River Heights and George in Deep River!

"He may have trailed us here," Bess worried. "If so, he'll hunt until he finds Nancy!"

George set her jaw. "If he does, you and I will run forward and help her!"

The man parked his car and went up to the front door. To the girls' surprise, he took a key from his pocket and let himself into the house.

Nancy, who had seen all this clearly, and fortunately had not been noticed, wondered if the stranger lived there. Again the thought went through her mind, "I've seen that man some place." As she tried hard to think where it had been, she heard voices in the room just above where she was crouched.

"Rudy Raspin!" exclaimed another man's voice. "Why did you come here in the daytime? You know we agreed that all our meetings would be at night."

"Listen, Oman," said Raspin, "don't give me orders. Things aren't going well. We'd better scram!"

A woman's voice said, "What happened?"

Before Raspin could answer, Oman broke in. But he had barely started to speak when the woman quickly ordered, "Be quiet, Ben! Listen to Rudy!"

"You're a nagging wife, Clara!" Oman complained.

Nancy's heart was thumping with excitement. Oman! The name on the postcard which had been found in Grandmother Horton's home! Also, Nancy was sure from the sound of Ben Oman's voice that he was Mr Seaman! So the man *was* using an alias!

Raspin went on, "Jake Suggs is in jail, and he has talked!"

Even outdoors Nancy could hear the gasps of alarm from the Omans. They asked what had happened.

"That pesky Drew girl and her friends searched the castle and found Suggs. I always said he was too dumb to be trusted. Well, they took him to the police. Then, a few hours later, Suggs told the cops about Mr Wheeler and they went out to the castle and rescued him."

"And now Wheeler will start talking!" Oman exclaimed in a thoroughly alarmed tone of voice. "We are in a tight spot."

His wife, who sounded doubtful about the story, asked, "Where did you get all this information, Rudy? You wouldn't have dared go to the jail to see Jake!"

"I wouldn't, eh?" Raspin asked in a sneering tone. "I'll tell you how I managed it. I just happened to go to that tearoom you like so much, and the old busybody there told me the story about Suggs being captured and Wheeler being found. Then I went to the jail."

Raspin laughed. "Pretty clever of me, too, the way I did it. I put on a disguise, and wrote a letter on stolen official state stationery I keep on hand along with other handy forms I pick up. The letter, addressed to Chief Burke, said I was a member of a state committee on jail inspection. I signed an assumed name."

"So you did talk to Suggs?" said Oman.

"Right. And I found out something else from him. Nancy Drew has my moonstone!"

"How'd she get it?" Ben Oman cried out, and his wife asked, "When did you learn that, Rudy?"

"Suggs told me. That fool held the Drew girl prisoner for a short time until he was discovered. Those girl friends of hers stood right outside the secret door on the castle cellar stairway. Suggs heard one of them say, 'That moonstone somebody sent her certainly didn't help Nancy.' "

Oman whistled, as Raspin, now in a loud and angry voice, said, "I don't know who sent it to her, but I have an idea. If I'm right, I'll—I'll—well, never mind, that's a personal matter. But I'm going to get the moonstone back! I've had bad luck ever since it disappeared!"

Nancy was amazed to hear that the moonstone she had received belonged to Rudy Raspin! Who had sent it to her? And why had it been taken from him?

After a few moments' silence, Raspin spoke again. "I tell you, it's getting too hot here. The sooner we get out, the better!"

"Just a minute," said Oman. "I'm not going to give up this job."

"You and Clara will be caught!" Raspin argued.

"Listen," said Ben Oman in a wheedling tone, "we have the old lady just where we want her. She's too weak to resist." The man laughed sardonically.

"That's right," spoke up Clara Oman. "She's signing cheques now without looking at them."

Rudy Raspin, apparently as greedy as his pals, laughed. "I guess we can't leave the loot behind," he said. "Well, force all you can out of the old lady's cheque book today. Tomorrow we get out of here!"

Nothing more was said and in a few moments Raspin left the house. As soon as he had driven off, Nancy cautiously returned to Bess and George and told the story. They stared in speechless amazement.

"We must get the police right away!" Nancy said. "Old Mrs Wilson is in real danger!"

The girls ran to Nancy's hidden car and hurried to town. As they neared the road leading up to the motel, she said, "I think it would be a good idea, before we go to the police, to see if there's any word from Dad."

When she reached the motel, the three girls dashed inside, all hoping for letters. There were none and no message from Mr Drew, but Mrs Thompson, who was behind the desk, said:

"Nancy, I found an envelope here this morning. The address looked so strange I thought I'd better keep the letter and hand it to you myself." She gave it to Nancy, then went off.

Nancy's name was spelled out in letters cut from newspaper words. Tied to the envelope was a small, dark-green box.

Remembering the package which contained the moonstone, Nancy quickly tore open the envelope and pulled out a note. It also was made from newspaper words. The message read:

> PLEASE RETURN MOONSTONE. NOW I
> AM IN DANGER AS WELL AS YOU. LEAVE
> IT IN THIS BOX TONIGHT UNDER THE
> RHODODENDRON BUSH AT THE FOOT OF
> THE MOTEL DRIVEWAY.

It was signed "The Well-Wisher".

Nancy showed the note to her friends, who gasped in astonishment. As the three girls walked away, Nancy said, "We'll leave the box tonight, but not the moonstone, and we'll be on watch to see who comes!"

19

A Cry for Help

As BESS peered at the strange note which Nancy had received, she said, "More than one person may come to get the moonstone back. And if they're husky men, we wouldn't stand a chance."

George looked at her cousin disdainfully. "Why not? We're not weaklings!"

"They might be armed," Bess cautioned.

Nancy thought only one person would appear. "I have an idea someone in the gang took the moonstone and sent it to me. We know now it actually belongs to Raspin, and I think he has ordered the person who sent the stone to get it back quickly."

"In any case, Nancy, you have stolen property," Bess said. "The quicker you get rid of it the better!"

Nancy agreed that the rightful owner should have the moonstone back, but thought Raspin should put in a claim for it himself.

"He wouldn't dare do that!" said Bess.

"Exactly," Nancy replied. "Therefore, we'll know that whoever comes tonight is in some way connected with Raspin."

George remarked that there was one fact still un-explained—why did this mysterious person call himself

"The Well-Wisher"? "That doesn't sound like one of the gang—rather a person who is on your side."

"I admit it's all very contradictory," said Nancy. "Let's hope we get the answers tonight."

The girls climbed into the convertible and went to police headquarters. Fortunately, Chief Burke was there and they were ushered into his office at once. As Nancy completed her story, the officer's eyebrows lifted in amazement.

"It certainly sounds as if you've stumbled on to a big fraud," he said.

"It may be bigger than we think," Nancy went on. "There are similarities between the way poor Mrs Wilson is being treated and the way Mrs Horton was some fifteen years ago."

"That's right," the chief said. "Do you think these servants are up to a racket that they've been pulling for some time?"

"It looks that way," Nancy replied.

On purpose Nancy refrained from saying anything about Joanie Horton—that was still her father's case.

The officer said he would send two squad cars out to Mrs Wilson's home at once. "I'll include a doctor because she may need medical attention."

Nancy asked, "May we go along?"

Chief Burke smiled. "I can't blame you for wanting to see this case through, but I don't want you to get hurt. Suppose you trail the police cars but stay in the background."

He went on to say that his men would confront the Omans with what Nancy had told him and he hoped for a confession from the couple. "Actually we have no conclusive evidence on which to arrest them, but maybe we can get some."

Nancy was glad that the two squad cars drove to Mrs Wilson's without using sirens or giving any other warning of their approach. She followed in her convertible. When the two dark saloon cars parked in the driveway, out of sight of the house, she stopped behind them.

In a short time the police had surrounded the old house. Tensely the three girls watched from behind the big trees along the driveway. A plain-clothesman went to the front door and lifted the knocker.

There was no answer. But suddenly the anxious group heard a faint cry for help!

"That must have been from Mrs Wilson!" said Bess, clutching Nancy's arm.

A few seconds later a loud order came from an upstairs room, "Be quiet and sign this!"

A woman's scream followed and another cry for help. Again the plainclothesman pounded loudly on the door, demanding, "Open up! Police!"

When there was no response to further commands, two other policemen and the doctor joined the plainclothesman. Together, they broke down the door with their shoulders. The men swarmed into the house.

The girls waited anxiously. "What do you suppose is happening in there?" Bess asked.

Nancy and George did not answer her. They were listening for further sounds from the house. Fully five minutes went by, and still they heard nothing.

Then the plainclothesman reappeared. "You can come in now," he called to the girls.

He led the way into the hall and up the front stairway. The detective indicated an open bedroom. Nancy and her friends entered.

"You!" a handcuffed man cried out. He was the person who had posed as Mr Seaman. He glared malevolently at Nancy.

The young sleuth ignored him and gazed at the two women in the room. One, evidently Mrs Oman, was also handcuffed.

On a large, old-fashioned bed lay an emaciated-looking elderly woman. The doctor sat beside her.

"This is Mrs Wilson," he said, and told her, "These are the girls who saved your life."

The woman smiled wanly and said in a weak voice, "I thank you. And I am glad these wicked servants have been caught."

The doctor said Mrs Wilson would be removed to a hospital and with proper food and good care would be all right. The police, meanwhile, had been examining things in the room. They had found an open cheque book from a New York City bank.

"Six of these cheques have been filled in—all for large amounts," said the officer in charge. "They are made out to various people with notations on the stubs to indicate purchases like antiques and a garden tractor which Mrs Wilson says she has not purchased."

"These dreadful people were trying to make me sign these cheques," the patient spoke up, almost in a whisper. "They plan to forge endorsement signatures and steal the money."

The detective asked Mrs Wilson how she happened to have such a sizable account in one bank.

"The Omans forced me to move my accounts from various savings banks," she answered. "They deposited them in one current account and all cheques were drawn from that."

The doctor gently patted the woman's hands. "Don't try to tell any more now," he said. "The police have enough evidence to take Mr and Mrs Oman to jail. When you feel better, you can testify against them."

Nancy and her friends said goodbye to Mrs Wilson, expressing the wish that she would recover soon from her ordeal. She smiled at them gratefully. "When I am feeling better, please come to see me. I want to thank you properly for all you have done."

The girls promised to do this, then left the room. They learned from the plainclothesman that the police would occupy the house and patrol the grounds to catch Rudy Raspin if he should return.

"He's supposed to arrive tomorrow," Nancy told the detective, "but I hope you won't have to wait that long."

The officers congratulated Nancy, Bess, and George for their work. The girls smiled in embarrassment, then went to the convertible.

"I wish we could find that awful Rudy Raspin," said Bess.

"So do I," Nancy agreed. "But right now our job is to find out who sent me the moonstone."

That evening the three girls left the little green box under the rhododendron bush at the foot of the motel driveway. Then they hid at various nearby points, with Nancy closest to the bush.

"We'd better keep still. No talking," she called to the

others. There was silence, except for the passing traffic

It grew darker and darker. No one came to th rhododendron bush. An hour went by and the girl began to fidget.

Cars sped by in both directions and occasionall entered the motel driveway. But no one stopped nea the rhododendron bush.

"Maybe the whole thing was a hoax," Georg thought.

Nancy had just begun to wonder whether the perso who had written the note had changed his mind abou coming, when a car speeding towards her pulled awa over to the side of the road and slowed down. I stopped a short distance from the rhododendron bush

The three girls tensed. They watched excitedly as th woman driver alighted. She walked forward quickly No one else was in the car. As she reached the rhodo dendron bush, the stranger dropped to her knees and started feeling around underneath it.

Nancy got ready to spring forward. The moment th woman picked up the box and rose to a standing position, Nancy jumped forward and beamed her flash light straight into her face. The next instant the youn; sleuth stepped back in amazement and cried out;

"Celia Smith!"

At once the woman knocked the flashlight from Nancy's hand, gave the girl a shove that pushed her t the ground, then ran towards her car!

20

Wolf's-eye Surprise

INSTANTLY Bess and George darted from their hiding places and grabbed the woman. She was surprised and fought them violently. But they pinned her arms back and held her tightly until Nancy could stand up, grab her flashlight, and come forward. This time she turned the light on herself.

"Nancy Drew!" the woman cried out.

Bess and George were astounded. "Do you know each other?" George asked.

"Yes," Nancy said quietly. "Celia was a day maid for my Aunt Eloise in New York for many years—in fact, until she married."

"Oh, Nancy, I'm so sorry I hit you," Celia Smith wailed. "I had no idea it was you speaking. When I sent you that moonstone, I was trying to save you from that dreadful gang. They're really after you! My husband is getting more and more desperate. He'll stop at nothing!"

"Who is your husband?" Nancy asked.

"Rudy Raspin."

"So that's why he looked vaguely familiar to me," the young sleuth said. "You once showed me a photograph of your fiancé but you never told me his name."

The girls now learned that Celia had been very unhappy since her marriage five years before. "Rudy's cruel and ruthless, but I was afraid to leave him. I learned what he and his friends are up to. He always said if I got him in trouble, he'd kill me!"

"You poor woman!" Nancy said sympathetically. "What is this racket?"

Celia replied that there were several couples in the group. One couple would talk a wealthy, usually elderly woman who had no relatives to look after her, into employing them as servants. "They always insisted that any other servants leave before their arrival. In this way the new employees never could be identified. The main idea was to rob the woman of as much as possible."

"And in some cases starve them to death!" said George.

Celia Smith looked at the girl in alarm. "Is that true?" she asked. "I'm sure my husband never resorted to that. But," she said, "the gang told me very little. They didn't trust me. Most of what I know I overheard. The gang threatened me a great deal—they were afraid, I guess, that I might go to the police."

"How long has this racket been going on?" Nancy asked.

"Oh, a long time."

"Was the first victim Mrs Horton?" Nancy inquired.

Celia Smith nodded. "That happened long before I married Rudy, but I found out about it. The Omans went there as servants. They learned that Mrs Horton's little granddaughter was being brought there by her other grandparents who were going to Africa. During the missionaries' short stay, the Omans were absent. They claimed that they were attending their daughter's wedding in New York.

"Clara Oman found out that Mrs. Horton was Joanie's only living relative outside of her maternal grandparents, so they planned that whole horrible kidnapping. It was carried out at the time of Mrs Horton's death. They gave the poor little girl a sedative to put her to sleep, then took her to the adoption society office and left her."

"Where is Joanie Horton now?" Bess asked.

"I don't know. And I'm sure my husband and the other members of the gang don't, either. I did find this out, though—they kept track of what happened to Mr and Mrs Bowen. When they returned from Africa and came here, Ben shadowed them. When they asked your father to take the case, Rudy was determined that Mr Drew was not going to learn the truth. Next, he found out from eavesdropping at your River Heights home that you girls were coming here to do some sleuthing. You have been in danger ever since."

"Oh!" exclaimed Bess.

"I took my husband's moonstone," Celia went on, "—he had brought it from Ceylon years ago and prizes it highly. I sent the stone to you, Nancy, with the note. You are so smart, I thought you would find out sooner or later the significance of the moonstone and Moonstone Valley."

Nancy said that it had taken her a long time to put the clues together and there were many questions still unanswered. "One of them is, where does the castle fit into the puzzle?"

"All I know is that they used it as a meeting place."

Suddenly Celia bit her lip and said with determination, "I'm never going back to Rudy Raspin! I don't care what happens to me—he is a wicked person, and I'm glad he has been found out. I'm sorry, Nancy, that I ever got mixed up in this racket. I should have gone to the police long ago."

"Suppose you tell me," said Nancy, "where they can find your husband."

Celia answered without hesitation. "We work for a senile, well-to-do old man, Mr Horace Boise, in the next town, Pleasantville."

Nancy invited Celia to come to the girls' room in the motel and talk further. "I'll go to your car with you and we'll drive it up to the motel's car park," she said. To George she murmured, "Call the police and tell them where they can find Raspin."

Ten minutes later Celia and the three girls met in the bedroom. Although Mrs Raspin was tearful, she looked relieved that at last she had followed her conscience. In answer to questions from Nancy, she revealed that it was her husband who had been chased from the Drew home by Detective Donnelly. He had hoped to break into the house and look for any papers on the Horton matter that might incriminate him.

Raspin also phoned Mr and Mrs Bowen in an attempt to keep Nancy from going to Deep River.

Oman had posed as Mr Seaman and given a phoney address to keep people from knowing where he worked. He had convinced Mrs Horton that her money would be safer in one large city bank, and her securities in a home safe, so she had transferred all her funds.

Mrs Oman had forged two notes in Grandmother Horton's handwriting. One gave a New York City address as that of her granddaughter. The other requested the private funeral. The note to Mr Wheeler was genuine, but the papers used by the fake Joan were forged by her mother.

Suggs had signalled messages to the Omans about visitors to the castle and when the police had made their inspection trips. He had also flooded the moat to keep visitors from the castle, but had not seen Nancy and George anchor the drawbridge and thought it was out of order.

"Have you any idea who took my car from the motel car park?" Nancy asked.

"Yes. Clara Oman did that, too. She and my husband were the ones who kidnapped Mr Wheeler. And it was Rudy who sent the note to Mrs Hemstead telling her you were using an assumed name. That was meant to scare you out of town. He tried to run down you and your friends in a boat, too."

About an hour later word came that the police of Pleasantville had taken Rudy Raspin into custody. He would be brought to Deep River the next day. Celia, nearly overcome by the whole affair, was put to bed at the motel. Nancy stayed with her, partly to care for the distraught woman, and partly to be sure she did not run away. Nancy knew the police would want to question her. In the morning two officers appeared and took Celia Raspin with them.

She had barely left when Nancy's father arrived with Mr and Mrs Bowen. They were overjoyed to hear the good news.

"We are glad our granddaughter is happy," said
Mrs Bowen. "And if the Armstrongs agree, we'd like to
talk with her."

Mr Bowen spoke up. "My wife and I have decided to
go back to Africa as missionaries. We want so much to
help underprivileged people."

"The Bowens have asked me," said Mr Drew, "what
I advise. I believe that Joanie should know the whole
story and that we should retrieve her stolen inheritance."

The lawyer went on to say that through the postcard
clue he had traced the Omans' daughter Claire in
California. "She admitted using phoney and forged
papers to impersonate Joanie. Claire claims she has
none of the inheritance left but she didn't sound very
sincere. I asked her a few leading questions and I'm
inclined to think her parents have retained the bulk of
the money."

Bess groaned. "But if they have it hidden away
they'll never tell where it is."

Suddenly Nancy's eyes sparkled. "I have a hunch as
to why the Omans and the rest of the thieves were using
the abandoned castle! To hide something! Girls, it's
perfectly safe out there now. Let's go and make a
real search!"

She asked her father if he wished to go along. Mr
Drew smiled but shook his head. "I must see the Armstrongs," he said. "You girls make your search and I'll
let you know later today what the rest of our plans will
be."

Excitedly the three girls set off in the convertible. On
the way to the castle they discussed what would be the
most likely hiding place for thieves to use.

"I'm sure it's the cellar," said Nancy. "You remember the only time we were warned away from the castle was when George and I swam over and started for the cellar."

This time the girls were armed with three flashlights, and the weird, dank passageway of the castle did not seem so forbidding. Their hunt revealed nothing until they came to what looked like a dungeon with a barred door. It was not locked and they went inside the cell-like room. Although they beamed their lights all round the walls, nothing suspicious was revealed.

"I think if there is anything hidden here it will be under this earthen floor," said Nancy. "It would be easy to dig up."

She sprawled full length on the ground. "What in the world are you doing?" Bess asked.

"Looking for a hump in the earth, even a slight one."

Suddenly Nancy stood up and dashed towards the corner of the dungeon. "Here's one!" she said. "Now what can we dig with?"

George remembered that she had seen a shovel in the old kitchen and hurried off to get it. She came back with the long-handled shovel, and at once began to dig. In a short time she uncovered a large brass box. Their pulses quickening, the girls lifted it out.

"You open it, Nancy," said George.

Nancy lifted the lid and the three girls gasped. The chest was filled with negotiable securities and money. Besides these, the girls found a list of people who had been swindled and also the names of two other couples in the gang.

"We'd better bury this again," Bess said, "and let the police come for it."

Before Nancy could answer, George protested, "No sir! After all the trouble we've had, I'm not going to let one of those crooks come here and take this fortune away!"

"I think you're right," said Nancy.

Since the chest was very heavy, all three girls helped to carry it to the car. Nancy drove at once to Deep River Police Headquarters. Chief Burke was amazed to receive the cache and said he would put it in his office safe at once.

"Then we'll round up those four other people in the gang whose names are on the list," he told the girls. "I have an idea that now the entire gang is accounted for."

Nancy smiled and thanked the chief for all his help. She did not tell him that there was still one matter to clear up—that of Jody Armstrong's reunion with her grandparents.

When Nancy and her friends reached the motel, they found Mr Drew, Mr and Mrs Armstrong, and the Bowens there. All looked very pleased.

Nancy's father, smiling, said, "The Armstrongs want Jody to meet Mr and Mrs Bowen tomorrow. They have invited the rest of us to come to their home after they've all spent an hour together."

The following day, when the Drews, Bess, and George arrived at the Armstrong home, they found an excited and happy group. Jody rushed up to the girls and hugged them.

"Oh, I have so many wonderful things to thank you for," she said. "And don't you think I'm about the

uckiest girl in the whole world to have such wonderful
adoptive parents and to have found these marvellous
grandparents? They've told me a number of things
about my mother and father who passed away when I
was very young—how they loved me and how happy
they would be to know I have such fine adoptive
parents."

"You certainly are fortunate," said Nancy, smiling.
"We're all so happy for you."

Mr Drew announced that about half of Grandma
Horton's stolen securities had been found intact in the
brass box at police headquarters and that in due course
Jody would receive it. The lawyer explained:

"What started the Omans on their kidnapping idea,
and having their own daughter pose as the Horton
beneficiary, was the fact that Ben Oman had seen a
copy of the will. The age of the granddaughter was not
mentioned, nor any guardian It was then that he began
formulating the fraud. He kept little Joanie out of sight.
Poor Grandma Horton was underfed and kept under
sedation until her death."

"How perfectly dreadful!" Bess said softly.

"Before a doctor was called to administer to her,"
Mr Drew went on, "Mrs Oman took little Joanie to the
adoption society and left her so no one coming to the
house ever saw her."

"How can people be so wicked!" George burst out.

Jody said that of course it would be very nice to
receive the money. "But I'm going to give a lot of it to
my grandparents to use in their work," she said. "Part
of what I have left will be for beautiful presents for
Nancy Drew, Bess Marvin, and George Fayne," she

declared. "They deserve the best rewards in the whole world!"

Nancy laughed. "That is sweet of you, Jody. But the only reward I want is to know what those strange code words 'Wolf's Eye' mean."

Jody went to the bookcase and began looking in dictionaries and encyclopaedias and other reference books. Nancy, meanwhile, could not help but wonder when she might encounter as strange a mystery as the the recent one.

Jody had been consulting one of the reference volumes which contained interesting information about all sorts of unusual subjects. Excitedly she cried out:

"I've found it!" Jody giggled. "Nancy, believe it or not, wolf's eye is a nickname for moonstone!"

Nancy Drew® Mystery Stories

by Carolyn Keene

Have you read all the books in this thrilling series?
Here are a few of the titles available:

The Clue in the Crossword Cipher (5)

Nancy travels to the mountains of Peru in search of price-
less treasure. But she soon discovers that an unknown
enemy is determined to stop her . . .

The Whispering Statue (14)

The eerie statue of the Whispering Girl points Nancy to an
ancient mystery that haunts the decaying Old Estate. But
horror awaits her in the night . . .

The Triple Hoax (51)

An invitation to a display of magic puts Nancy on the
track of a ruthless gang of con men. But she soon realizes
that the tricksters are dangerous criminals . . .

The Silver Cobweb (65)

A mysterious spider symbol is Nancy's only clue to a jewel
robbery. But she quickly becomes enmeshed in a terrifying web of danger . . .

Armada

SUPERSLEUTHS

by FRANKLIN W. DIXON and CAROLYN KEENE

A feast of reading for all mystery fans!

At last, the Hardy Boys and Nancy Drew have joined forces to become the world's most brilliant detective team

Together, the daredevil sleuths investigate seven spine chilling mysteries: a deadly roller-coaster that hurtles to disaster, a sinister bell that tolls in a city of skeletons, a haunted opera house with a sinister curse — and many more terrifying situations.

Nancy Drew and the Hardy Boys — *dynamite!*

Armada

LINDA CRAIG
MYSTERIES
by ANN SHELDON

Linda Craig loves horses — and adventure! Together, she and her beautiful palomino pony, Chica d'Oro, find themselves caught up in all kinds of dangerous escapades — chasing cut-throat horse thieves through underground caverns, roaring down mountain passes after death-dealing smugglers, treasure hunting in the burning desert — and much more. Make sure you don't miss Linda's action-packed adventures.

If you like Nancy Drew, you'll love Linda Craig!

Armada

Armadas are chosen by children all over the world. They're designed to fit your pocket, and your pocket money too — and they make terrific presents for friends. They're colourful, exciting, and there are hundreds of titles to choose from — thrilling mysteries, spooky horror stories, hilarious joke books, brain-teasing puzzles, fascinating hobby books, stories about ponies and schools — and many, many more. Armada has something for everyone.

Book Tokens

Give them the pleasure of choosing

Book Tokens can be bought and exchanged at most bookshops

Armada